MI NEVA KNOW SEY

BY
ERICA MCKOY- HIBBERT

MI NEVA KNOW SEY

BY
ERICA MCKOY- HIBBERT

MACHIBB CREATIONS
Publishing House
West Milford, New Jersey

Copyright 1999 by Erica McKoy- Hibbert
All rights reserved. No part of this book may be reproduced in any form or by any means, without prior written permission of the author.

Published by Machibb Creations Publishing House
27 Hancock Drive, West Milford, NJ 07480
973 697-4079

ISBN 1-930331-2

Library of Congress Catalog Card Number:
99-97828

Cover Illustration: Erica McKoy- Hibbert

Cover Design: Grace Largie- Pringle
Howell, NJ

Edited by: Patricia Booth
Far Rockaway, NY

Book Layout: Amy Cahill

NEW YORK, 2000
PRINTED IN THE UNITED STATES
By: RJ COMMUNICATION
51 E.42ND ST. NYC, NY 10017

Melody Pennycook's adventure evokes strong feelings of my own life in America and Jamaica. A must read for all West Indians whom I'm sure can identify with Melody. Also for non-West Indians who, like Melody, have experienced the diaspora. A Profoundly well-written book which captures not only the teenage spirit but the spirit of the Caribbean adult life also. Erica has come into her own as a dynamic writer. Congratulations to my good friend whom I have known and admire over the years.

PEARLINE BLACKWOOD
ESQUIRE, NY,NY-IMMIGRATION LAW

Mi Neva Know Sey, Erica McKoy Hibbert's first book, conveys the essence of youthful expectations. The reader especially immigrant females, cannot help but recall their own youth- full of hopes, dreams and ambitions. Like Melody Pennycook, Hibbert's main character, most immigrants have experiences in their adopted countries that prove beyond compare. Like Melody, they can file these in a folder, in their lives labeled, "Mi Neva Know Sey". Melody Pennycook is the epitome of the immigrant teenaged schoolgirl.

Patricia Boothe
Editor- At Large, EVERYBODY'S Caribbean Magazine

Melody Pennycook is a challenger, through fears and uncertainties, she survives all that a new country can tender her. Erica Mckoy-Hibbert, like her main character is also a challenger, venturing out on her first novel. I have worked with Erica during her graduate studies at Montclair and I immediately recognized her writing abilities. I thoroughly enjoyed the story and learned a few things about Jamaica. Let's hope that Erica will make this book, the first of many to come.

Dr. David Weischadle –author of ("228" A Novel)
Professor and Dept Advisor- Montclair State University

In Memory of the Late
Lena A. McKoy
December 16, 1927 to October 19, 1993

TABLE OF CONTENTS

ACKNOWLEDGMENT.. *viii*
AUTHOR'S NOTE.. *ix*
BOOK QUOTE... *x*
FOREWORD... *xi*

PROLOGUE..1

PART ONE
GOODBYE JAMAICA..6
FACING THE CHALLENGE...15
TROUBLE IS COMING..33
UNDERSTANDING THE DIFFERENCES.....................40
AH SCHOOL..55

PART TWO
SCHOOL SHOCK...76
A WONDERFUL AMERICAN EXPERIENCE...............83
CHURCH NO PROBLEM...98
A FEELING OF BELONGING.....................................102
LOVING THE AMERICAN ADVENTURE................111
COPING WITH JERRON...117

PART THREE
ENOUGH IS ENOUGH-IT'S THE HOLIDAYS............120
A PLEASANT BEGINNING..127
A SPIRITUAL AWAKENING......................................131
IN RETROSPECT...134

AFTERWARD...139
GLOSSARY..141

Acknowledgement

I am truly grateful to everyone who, through his/her contribution played a special part in the making of this novel. To all, I say thank you. To write a novel was a dream I had for many years and today that dream is a reality.

To my husband, Barry Hibbert, my two sons, Barrington Clayon (BC) and Triston DiShawn, thanks for your support. Barry, thanks for being my first (free) editor; reading the first draft and giving me your honest feedback. Thanks for helping me find/restore the documents, the times when I had some major problems. Barrington Jr., 'BC'. Thanks for being my audience when I read certain scenes, and I wanted to know if the lines were clear: you understood exactly what I was saying by dramatizing the part. Thanks for giving me pointers on the American lingo, so I could do the dialogue just right. Triston, thanks for being my school reference; confirming the facts about school life when I wasn't quite sure.

A special thanks to all my family, (brothers and sisters) for the love we share with each other: for the bond we have cherished all these years. To my editor, Patricia Booth, of Far Rockaway, New York. Thanks for working with me, fitting into my schedule. Your editing skills are in order. Noelle Miles and Rose Sharon Green, of Paterson, my computer wizards. Thanks for all your computer assistance and expertise. To my proof-reader, Jeffrey D. Present, Esq. of New York. Thanks for taking time out of your busy schedule to assist in this project.

Lyndel Young- Roberts, my high school English teacher. Thanks for making me think harder- even when I thought I did my best. It paid off. To my artist, Grace Largie – Pringle, your artwork says exactly what I need to demonstrate. And I cannot leave your husband, D'Angelo out, so to you 'D', I say thanks for the part you played.

Last, but definitely not the least, a big thank you to my mother, the late Lena Atterbury- McKoy. My friend, my support through all those years until she said goodbye to me. For all her love and the sacrifices she made, which helped me, be who I am today. To my mother I dedicate this book.

Love You All

Author's Note

This is a work of fiction. Any references to actual events, real people, or real locales are only a figment of the author's imagination, intended to give the novel a sense of reality and authenticity. Names, characters, places and incidents are either a product of the author's imagination or used fictitiously and any resemblance to real life is purely coincidental.

"MI NEVA KNOW SEY"

" THE CREDIT BELONGS TO THOSE WHO ARE ACTUALLY IN THE ARENA….. IF THEY FAIL, FAIL WHILE DOING GREATLY, SO THAT THEIR PLACE SHALL NEVER BE WITH THOSE COLD, TIMID SOULS WHO KNOW NEITHER VICTORY NOR DEFEAT."
THEODORE ROOSEVELT- 1901- 1909

Foreword

The 1992 Statistical Yearbook reports that from the years 1901 to 1990, there were approximately 38 million legal immigrants to the USA. The Immigration and Naturalization Service Statistics reveal that in 1996, there were approximately five million undocumented aliens residing in the United States.

'Peoples the world' over, the twentieth century, pulled up stakes and immigrated to the US shores in droves. Aided by television, and in the last decade of this century, by the information superhighway, citizens in this global village have yearned to experience a bit of Americana.

Prior to leaving our respective countries, many of us have romanticized the American experience. However, when the opportunity comes to emigrate from our country to the USA, there is usually a cognitive dissonance between our perceptions, and the realities of everyday life in this "melting pot". Yet, these incongruities have not prevented the flow of immigration: and immigration continues unabated. Immigrants have learned to make the necessary adjustments and, by and large, have successfully assimilated into this society.

The narrative that follows, "Mi Neva No Sey", is one such saga. It is a story of a young girl who moved to the United States to be with her parents who had earlier made a new life in America. In many ways the story is typical; parents leave Jamaica to come to the United States to make a better living, and as soon as possible, sponsor their children to join them. In another important way, this story is atypical in that the narrative deals with the issues from the vantage point of a teenager, who through no choice of her own, is thrust into this strange milieu and must find effective coping mechanisms.

The author of this novel scrupulously tracks the life of this well adjusted child, who is suddenly uprooted from the warmth of her friends, her grannyma, as well as the loving embrace of her sunny Jamaica, to the stressful churning of city-life in the Big Apple. Melody's feelings could best be characterized as mixed. For her, it could be said it was the "best of times and the worst of times". She was buoyant with the prospect of seeing her mother again, yet torn to the core with the thought leaving her grannyma. She was shaken with the realities of leaving the familiar, but yearned to discover new things. She would miss her old friends deeply, but perhaps she could make new American friends.

The narrative is a remarkable demonstration of the human spirit that enables one to cope, even under unusual and threatening circumstances. The reader's heart will be warmed by Melody's resilience and resourcefulness. It will soon become obvious how Melody's spirituality sustains her in times of crisis.

The perceived value of a literary work is often measured by its commercial success, so on that measure only, time will tell whether or not Erica Mckoy-Hibbert's first novel is a success. However, on the basis that this work appeals to the better part of us and inspires us to persevere against the odds, it is already a success in my mind. My hope is that you will concur.

Congratulations to Erica on a fine work.

Contributed By: Barrington C. Hibbert
BSC, Organizational Management
MS, Human Resource Management
MS, Technology Management

I LEAVE BUT I WILL ALWAYS STAY,
WHILE MEMORIES OF HOME
LIKE GREEN GRASS LAY.
I TAKE MY FLIGHT AND UTTER A SIGH,
AND LOOK AWAY
AS LOVED ONES WAVE SAD GOODBYES.

OUT INTO A NEW WORLD I GO,
TO A PLACE AND PEOPLE I DO NOT KNOW.
I AM HAPPY, I AM SAD.
I AM FRIGHTENED, I AM GLAD.
I LAUGH, I CRY. I CLOSE MY EYES.
I THINK……..AND I WONDER WHY.

A FAREWELL SONG
ERICA MCKOY-HIBBERT -1987

Prologue

She is not brown. Nor can she be referred to as a mulatto. She is more white than fair. And all who know her refer to her as Miss Lilieth, fair grand pickney. Her hair is between a shade of brown and bronze and is of a curly, wavy texture. When she was a young child, her hair would not stay plaited unless Grannyma knotted the ends with rubber bands. Now, as she grows older, a missy girl in her prime, she combs her own hair, creating different styles, and parades in front of the round-faced bureau mirror in her small bedroom.

Her favorite style for school is making a part in the middle of her hair, from her forehead to the nape of her head. She then makes two big plaits held together by a clip at each end. Sometimes, when she is late for school, she scoops her brown-bronze hair into one fluffy bundle with a round ponytail clip, and leaves it hanging loosely to bounce in the heat of the sun. When she combs her hair like this, it is obvious that she is mixed. Mixed with white blood.

The day she was born in the small one bedroom house on Lucky Lane in Kingston, her mother had looked at the new baby-girl after the pain had subsided and cradled her to her milk-laden breast. The sound of the baby-girl's father's voice still echoed in her mother's ear, and the memory of his melodious Irish accent brought a smile to her face, as she looked at her white-skinned daughter. "Melody," she said, in whisper. "Me naming you Melody." She gave her newborn daughter her last name, and not that of her father's, because he had been gone now for almost a year and she knew she would never see him again. She wanted to bury the past in any way she could and take care of her beautiful, fair daughter. The exclusion of her father's name would make it easier for her.

Bubbles, Melody's older sister, was either jealous, or feisty; Melody was not really sure. Bubbles ridiculed her many times when they fussed with each other, saying things like, "Go weh! You sailor pickney yuh."

In their confrontations, Melody would throw back some insults: "And look pon fe yuh negar head, it picky, picky like wha."

Although Bubbles was the instigator, she could not handle the payback and a physical fight would ensue. It was not a vicious, brutal street fight, but enough to cause the punches and the scratches to leave black and blue marks on Melody's fair skin. Their grandmother always seemed to notice the bruises, eventually, and wanted to know if they were from a street fight or not.

"Mel, is what happen to you face, child?" she would ask.

Melody would attempt to lie, but her grandmother could read her like she read the Psalms at night.

"Don't lie to me, little girl. You and yuh sister fighting again, nuh. Tell me! No! Do! What now?"

"Is she first start, mam. She call me . . . ," Melody would reply, stopping short, as her grandmother interrupted.

"How much time a must tell unoo not to fight over who you are. No color, no hair, nothing, eeh! The fact remains unoo still sisters, same mother, same womb. It doesn't matter who de father is. Is the same cord dat give the both of yuh life to born."

She was serious as she chided her younger granddaughter. Melody used to be embarrassed and sorrowful when her grandmother scolded her.

"But . . . but," Melody stuttered.

"No, but nothing; go bring yuh sister come here right now!"

In a minute, both girls were before their counselor for the umpteenth time and received a proper scolding. For a few hours, they walked at a distance from each other with pouting lips and *cut their eyes* at one another when they were within close range. But not long after, they would become the best of friends again.

* * * * * *

Melody sits on the small porch of her house on Prospect Street in Brooklyn. It is a beautiful Friday afternoon. The temperature is unseasonably cool although it is late June. It is the last week before the 1980 summer holidays for the New York City School District. Melody, a new-comer to Brooklyn, watches the children walk home from school and imagines herself doing the same thing as of September. She makes a keen observation of the children and notes that none of them is wearing a school uniform. This, she concedes will be one of her new changes -- going to school without a uniform.

She also watches as some children play on the sidewalk and listens to the sirens of speeding police cars as they whiz by constantly. As she notices the many different races of people in the street going about their business, a thought crosses her mind: "Did my father come from America. Will I ever run into him? No one has ever told her where he came from; she was only told he was from *foreign*. She always thought of America as foreign when she was back home in Jamaica, and now here she was. How would she manage? Would she like America? She had just recently begun her new life in a very big city, in a very big country.

As she stares into oblivion, she whispers to herself: "Time will tell, because dem always seh, 'see me and come live wid me a two different things.'"

From her vantage point on the porch, Melody sees a man walking his dog which is constrained by a leash. The dog (a half German shepherd) tries to pull away from his master's hold and stops in front of the brownstone, lifts his right foot and relieves himself against the wall. He then stoops and relieves himself again on the sidewalk. The man looks around, nervously, then tugs on the leash and steps off in a hurry. Melody smiles scornfully, "Nasty dog! No, not really. Is a nasty man! Mek the dog make him mess right at the people gate."

The mere sight of the dog and his dedicated master leaves an indelible impression in Melody's mind. It is her first evidence that America will bring many new experiences. Based on what she has just observed, she makes a comparison with Jamaican dogs. Since coming to America, Melody has learned that dog owners must abide by the law and curb their dogs. Back in Jamaica, most dogs run wildly on the streets, stray in different places and relieve themselves with no thought or respect towards anyone . . . on the street, in anyone's yard, or on their verandah. They are not chaperoned by anyone and, as a matter of fact, are at risk if they come in contact with boys.

Melody recalls that most boys in Jamaica test their aiming skills at dogs. When the missile -- a small rock -- reaches its target -- the dog's belly or face -- the animal's response is a pitiful, howling scream which can be heard from a distance. A dog is nothing but a *dawg* in Jamaica, and hardly ever on a leash. She remembers always begging her cousin Novand not to bother the dogs when they used to walk to the shop together. As Novand ran to find a rock, he would say, "Gimme a big rockstone mek mi lick dah dawg deh." He always seemed to find the rock before Melody's pleas could have an impact on him, and the howling cry from the dog always rang in her ear and heart.

Melody closes her eyes and shakes her head pitifully as she reflects. She remembers the dogs' pain even now as she thinks about the incidents. Dogs in Jamaica are not catered to like dogs in America, who seem to get a lot of respect. In fact, Melody recalls, when someone wants to bring you down, they compare you to a dog. They'll say, "Go weh, yuh walk 'bout like dawg" or "Go weh, you dawg you." Or when one wants to infer that another is poverty-stricken and malnourished, the comparison is made to an undesirable looking dog, as in, "Look pon yuh, yuh fava mawga dawg." From what Melody has seen in television commercials in America, dogs are treated like a member of the family. They are cared for, treated well and loved. On television, she has seen how some dogs practically sleep in the same bed with their owners. Dogs in America eat good, nutritious food and go to the veterinarian for check- ups. When she first accompanied her Mom to the supermarket, she noticed there was an entire aisle stacked with dog and cat food. There was even a choice of dog food for puppies or grown dogs. She had read the ingredients listed on the label of a can of Purina Chow and saw that it was loaded with good stuff. "Bwoy," she had mused, "America really plentiful and rich feh true. It has a lot of opportunity for both man and dog."

Melody shakes herself out of her reverie. The man she saw walking his dog is a true American. He allows his pet, his best friend, to drag him in every direction. Melody notices other dogs and masters pass by, as if they are taking part in a parade. America so far, she admits, is an interesting place to be.

Many thoughts race through her mind. There is a lot to see, to know and to learn in her new environment. Is she prepared? Can she handle it? Her greatest apprehension is the adjustment to her new school life. But, again, she consoles herself. "Time will tell."

She gets up from the oval wicker chair, stretches her long hands over her head and yawns. She is sleepy. She goes into the room she shares with her sister Bubbles and falls across the twin bed. Her eye catches the poster of the Jamaican Coat of Arms she had brought with her from Jamaica for a souvenir. *'Out of Many One People'*, reads its motto. She immediately thinks of her grandmother and best friend back in Jamaica. As she drifts off to sleep, she wonders what her grandmother is doing and chuckles at a joke her best friend, Retinella, had told her.

So ends Melody's first week in the city of Brooklyn, New York.

The week had yielded new experiences, fears and anxieties. Being in America has been an eye-opener. Thirteen-year-old Melody Pennycook has one of two choices: she can return to Jamaica to live with her grandmother or stay and face the challenges in America. Her immediate gut feeling tells her she must stay.

PART ONE

Goodbye Jamaica

It is the first of June, and already the sun is spreading its burning rays over the island of Jamaica, on Spanish Town, a small but busy town on the outskirts of the capital city, Kingston. The small three-room house on Peanut Lane is full of excitement. There is plenty of movement as the two sisters, Melody and Bubbles, scurry from room to room trying to get themselves ready. They still cannot believe that the day has finally arrived when they are going to America to live with their mother and step-father, who has legally adopted them.

It has been almost ten years since their mother, Anel Marks, migrated to the United States. She left Jamaica a single woman but after three years in America, she met and married Winston Pennycook. He too is a Jamaican who has lived in America for three years prior to Anel's arrival. Melody and Bubbles move back and forth in the house.

"Grannyma, I can't find my white pantyhose stockings Miss Nel sent for me for Christmas. Mi put it right over by mi bed head and now mi can't find it, mam." Melody is excited about her pending trip but, at the same time, a feeling of uncertainty weighs on her mind.

"Look if it drop under the bed or something, nuh!" Grannyma knows her granddaughter is happy, excited and nervous, all at the same time.

"Yes, Grannyma, ah find it, mam."

"Melody where is mi black shoes. You move it last night from where I put it, nuh?"

Bubbles, too, is excited but she is not worried about leaving Jamaica. She cannot wait to join her two best friends who left Jamaica two years ago to live in New Jersey and Connecticut, respectively. She knows that she will be living in Brooklyn, New York, but her distance from them will now be so much closer.

"Why are you accusing me that I take up your shoes, Bubbles? Why would I want to do *that*?" Both girls laugh as Melody emphasizes the word 'that' in an imitation American accent.

"Melody and Bubbles, unoo almost ready? Ah don't want to mek Mister Rupert come and wait on us, you nuh," Grannyma yells from the detached wood frame kitchen. She is busily wrapping up some cerasee, black mint and other Jamaican goodies to send for her daughter, Anel.

Mister Rupert, a good friend of Grannyma's, has volunteered to take the family to the airport on the morning of the sisters' departure, and she does not want him to have to wait.

Grannyma then goes into the house to get dressed. The ceiling fan is making more noise than cooling the small house. Grannyma hums a quiet tune as she dresses for the trip to the Norman Manley Airport. "*Under the Blood, the Precious blood, Keep me Savior, from day to day, under the Precious Blood.*" She, like Melody and Bubbles, is happy that the girls are going to join their mother. But she is already sad that she will be living alone until she finds someone to live with her. She probably will get one of her sister's grandchildren.

* * * * * *

Lilieth Atterburn, the girls' grandmother, is affectionately called *Grannyma* even by those who are not family members. She was married to Knutsford Marks at the early age of twenty and the union produced one daughter, Anel. An older daughter, Pansy, her husband's child, went to live with her mother in England, but later migrated to the United States. Grannyma has been a widow for over fifteen years since Knutsford's death. Her daughter Anel and two granddaughters, Melody and Bubbles, are her life. She never remarried and occupied her time with raising her daughter, then her two granddaughters. Her role as surrogate mother to Bubbles and Melody commenced when they were babies.

Bubbles, who is almost a year and half older (seventeen months) than her sister Melody, was actually born in Grannyma's house, then a two-room apartment. Melody was brought to her when she was eleven months old. After Bubbles was born, Anel went to live in Kingston, where she hoped to find night work so she could afford the tuition for commercial school.

Anel found a job working in a bar and, although working as a bar maid was not her first choice, it was a job that could support her daughter and herself. The bar, the "Blue Moon," was one of the popular taverns in town. It was located on Seabrink Road and was a haven for the many sailors who alighted from the ships that docked in the Kingston harbor.

Melody was conceived in this environment. Her dad, an Irish

Admiral, Patrick Courtleigh Fennigan, was a tall and handsome man with brown, wavy hair. He had come in on the Dubliner from Ireland, two days before visiting the Blue Moon. Admiral Fennigan was sitting at a table with three other sailors, drinking and having fun, as Anel, their hostess for the five hours they were there, catered to their needs. They sat drinking Appleton rum, glass after glass, and each time Anel served their table, she could feel Fennigan's stare as she replaced the used glasses with clean ones. The third time she went over, he asked her name, and she responded bashfully.

"Anel." He teased. "How beautyiful!" His Irish accent was very melodious and it made her blushed. He was also a little drunk.

On his third visit to the tavern, a Friday, Patrick asked her to take him to a popular Jamaican eating spot. At first, she was shy and afraid of the gossip that she knew would come from her date with a sailor, but she accepted after he pleaded with her.

"C'mon Anel, I will be here for a whole five weeks. Got to know me way 'round, eh? Need to know all the nice places in town. Don't you say, me lassie?"

She hated the name *lassie*, but his accent intrigued her and she knew that it was his European culture that made him refer to her as a lassie. The following Friday night when she was off from work, they drove in his rental car to a nice bamboo-built restaurant, the "Fish Dish," out on the St. Thomas Road. The "Fish Dish" was famous for the tasty fish cooked a variety of ways and served with delicious steamed bammy.

The first time alone with Patrick was enjoyable and she yearned to be with him every chance she got, although she knew he would only be around for another month.

Then, it happened! Three weeks before he left. They had gone to another place to eat outside of the Old Harbour area with his two buddies. This time, he did not drive but sat in the back seat of the car with Anel on the way to the restaurant. After eating and drinking for a few hours at the "Nyam And Go Weh" roadside restaurant, they headed back to Kingston. As they neared the hotel where Patrick was staying, he said to Anel, "Mighty jolly if you could come up to my pad for a while."

Butterflies danced in her stomach. She wanted to say, "yes," without thinking about it, but she looked at him questioningly before answering.

He sensed her hesitation. "Don't be afraid me, luv, Patrick won't bite, you know. I just want you to chat with me a bit. You tell me all about yourself and Jamaica. Aye."

"He does it all the time," she thought to herself. His accent always seemed to hypnotize her, and she yielded. She knew he was a bit drunk but it did not matter. She stayed all night.

One week before he left, she knew for sure, and she had two choices, either to abort the child she was carrying or carry it to term. When "The Dubliner" set sail that Sunday morning, Anel decided to keep her baby and accepted the fact that neither of them would see this man again. The father of her unborn child. She had not told him, and he did not know, that a child would be born to him in the island of Jamaica where he had made a stop when he left Ireland.

She stood at the dock that morning, touched her stomach and, in a whisper, said, "Goodbye, Mr. Irishman, what you don't know won't hurt you. Me no think it would, anyway."

She sat for a while and stared at the sprays of the beautiful blue sea, then she went home to her one room apartment on Lucky Lane. Two months later, when she began to experience morning sickness and felt sick when she went to work and smelled the liquor, Anel contemplated abortion again. She was upset. She was confused and she was ashamed. "Wha' Mama gwine seh? What people gwine think. Lawd help me! Look what me do to meself. At least Bubbles' Daddy is here in Jamaica and me and she can find him if we want, but me know seh meh never going to see this white man again."

She covered her face with her hands and the tears poured down her face like raindrops falling from a zinc roof. The following Saturday morning, she got dressed to go on a mission. She was going to see the woman in Mango Walk her friend Baby Love told her about. She boarded the Mayflower bus that was headed for the country and sat by the window. Tears welled up in her eyes and she closed them to hold back the tears. Soon she was asleep. She had worked into the wee hours of Saturday morning and had no sleep before she set out on her mission.

Anel never made it to Mango Walk because the bus didn't stop where she should have gotten off. She had been still asleep and was unable to alert the driver. When the bus reached the terminal, she got off and took the next bus back to Kingston. She returned home that day, convinced that missing her stop was a sign that she was about to do the wrong thing. She resigned herself to carrying the baby to term and concealed the pregnancy from her mother until the day the baby was born. Eleven months later, when she needed help, Melody, like her sister, was given to Grannyma to raise.

Grannyma remembers the incident as if it only happened yesterday.

* * * * * *

Satisfied that she is well adorned for her grandchildren's departure, Grannyma picks up the black handbag her daughter had sent her, then looks in the mirror to admire herself. A sly grin brightens her face as she muses upon Melody's going to America. "She will blend right in. At least sorta blend in wid the white 'Merican dem, cause she has fair skin plenty."

Grannyma remembers the day clearly, thirteen years ago, when Anel brought the child to her. When she laid eyes on the baby, she could tell that the father was not a Jamaican black man and also that he was not a Jamaican fair-skinned man. She was certain the father of her second grandchild was a foreign white man off the ship.

Still reflecting on the past, Grannyma smiles and moves towards the verandah. As she is about to sit down on the plastic lounge chair there, she hears a horn tooting. It is Mister Rupert, on time as usual, to take them to the airport.

"Gal pickney, come on, Mister Rupert is here. Bring out all the bags so 'im can start packing them up in the trunk," she calls out to her granddaughters.

Bubbles and Melody bring out their luggage and the packages they are taking with them to America. Melody has more pieces than Bubbles because she has packed most of her school books; she has even packed the last tunic she wore to Chenrt All Age School. She wants to hold on to these items for posterity so that the memory of her thirteen years in her homeland will never be erased from her mind.

Mister Rupert and Dudley, his nephew, pack the trunk of the Ford Cortina which seems too small to hold all the suitcases, let alone carry five people. But they do fit. It is truly amazing how Jamaicans seem to use the smallest and simplest resources to accomplish their needs, like fitting so many bags and people in such a small vehicle.

The girls wave their final goodbyes to all their friends, relatives and neighbors who gathered to wish them well on their journey. A small group has gathered in and around the yard. Some are standing at the door of their homes, while others stand at their gates. Some look on from across the barb-wired fence.

Retinella Roper is still talking to Melody as Mister Rupert shifts the car into first gear. "Member fe write, yuh nuh, Mel. Don't forget me, for yuh is still mi best friend."

"Yes, man, mi wi write yuh every day. Ah won't forget you atall, Retti," Melody promises. The two girls look at each other and tears fill their eyes, as Mister Rupert drives off.

After getting into the Kingston area, Mr. Rupert takes the short route down Four Shore Road to reach to the furthest point on Windward Road. He then picks up the Norman Manley Airport Road outside of Harbour View and heads for the airport.

Melody looks at the mountains on both sides of the road and admires the blue Caribbean Sea as she passes Gunboat Beach. She feels a knot in her throat. She is happy, but she is also sad. She is leaving her homeland, her roots. Melody sighs, "Ah, well, me wi see!"

Although America is considered to be the land of opportunity, a country where many people crave to be, for a thirteen-year-old girl leaving her homeland, it brings a feeling of consternation. Yet, if the truth is told, the Diaspora can be very challenging for anyone, and Melody too, anticipates challenges for herself.

"Are you all right, mama?" Bubbles asks Melody, with a sound of concern in her voice.

Bubbles is not sad at all. Her thoughts are of the splendor, the luxuries and the fashions America has to offer her. She had spent most of her life dreaming of going to America, the country she knows only by reputation from the various media.

They arrive at the airport and, after checking in, there is about twenty minutes before boarding time. Grannyma takes the opportunity to chat with them and give her counsel one last time. "A beg unoo, please be good. Good to yuhself and yuh parents. Don't get mix up with nothing bad. No bad company, you hear me! 'Merica has a whole heap of good things to offer. But just try to get all the good things the decent way," she admonishes.

She gives Bubbles a challenging look of scrutiny, then looks at

Melody, ruefully. But their time together is soon cut short by the announcement for boarding: *"All passengers for Flight 553, please proceed to Gate 4."* The sisters kiss and embrace their grandmother, then walk out into the hot sun to make their climb onto the big aircraft that stands on the runway.

Melody and Bubbles find their seats and settle in. Melody has the window seat and is grateful for this, since she'll be able to turn her face away from Bubbles if she becomes too overwhelmed. The window seat will allow her to conceal the gloom on her face when sadness creeps upon her.

The aircraft begins to taxi away from the building and the waving crowd grows smaller and smaller. Soon, the plane begins to make its ascent into the air. Both girls feel a bit nervous since this is their first time in an airplane. Yet, they are comforted by the prayer their grandmother had said earlier that morning, asking for their safe journey.

Melody looks at the landscape below her as the aircraft soars higher and higher. The island she had lived on for thirteen years, for the first time, appears very small. She is, of course, aware of its size; only 4,411 square miles, according to her geography text book.

A short time later, the captain's voice sounds over the intercom: "Ladies and gentlemen, we are now flying over the island of Cuba. If you look to your left, you will see the island."

Bubbles stretches across Melody to peep through the tiny window. Melody, a bit startled and nervous, pulls back from the window.
"You fraidie fraidie, eeh, Mel? Castro not going to do anything," Bubbles taunts her sister. She assumes that Melody is thinking about all the things she has heard about the neighboring island, just 90 miles from Jamaica; the talks about its strict totalitarian regime, and the rigid control of its leader, Fidel Castro.

"Me not fraidie nothing, me just giving you space to look," Melody responds to Bubbles' taunt, and musters a smile. She is indeed guilty of her sister's allegations and knows Bubbles cannot be fooled.

They both laugh. Melody pulls a magazine from the pocket of the seat in front of her and begins to read. Bubbles opens her Mills and Boon Romance novel and she too starts to read. Within the half hour, both girls fall asleep.

About an hour later, they are awakened by the sound of the flight attendant's voice. She speaks quietly but loud enough for them to hear. "Are the ladies eating, today?"

"Ye . . . Yes, mam. We are eating, mam", Melody says, a bit disoriented, as she peeps out the window and realizes they are still in the air.

"Wha . . . what you seh?" Bubbles is still drowsy, as she turns to look at the attendant.

Lunch consists of mashed potato, a quartered piece of roast chicken and a small slice of chocolate cake. They eat heartily, realizing that they are very hungry. They had only drank a mug of green tea and ate some crackers with butter, early that morning, before they left for the airport.

After eating, they feel more comfortable and relaxed.

"Lawkes, Mel! You clean you plate!" Bubbles teases her sister.

"Like you any better," Melody quips. They both laugh and recline their seats to comfortable positions.

The flight takes them across the Caribbean Sea and up to the Bahamian Islands. Suddenly, they begin to experience some turbulence, and Melody and Bubbles grab their seats and close their eyes tightly. The turbulence lasts for about five to eight minutes and both pray, silently, that God will guide them safely through the rest of their journey.

After another thirty minutes, the captain announces that they are flying above the mainland of America. He tells the passengers that they are flying over the state of Florida, the most southeastern tip of the United States and that the path for the remaining route up to New York would take them over the Eastern seaboard. He also promises that the rest of the journey should be smooth.

The flight is smooth and relaxing for the rest of the journey, during which both girls resume their reading. Occasionally, they peak through the window to view portions of the vast country of America, which appears to move beneath the aircraft, while the captain keeps them informed of the path. The aircraft starts its descent soon after it passes over New Jersey, and makes its entry into New York City. Bubbles and Melody grow excited at the sight of the tall buildings reaching high into the sky and cluttered together. From their vantage point, New York looks like a walled city. The view is occasionally blurred by the fog and smog polluting the air, but this does not hamper their joy.

"A bet you seh the streets dem clean and everything nice," says Bubbles, elated.

"Maybe. But me no think seh all over clean and nice atall," replies Melody, trying to be realistic and calm.

"It Big! Big! though and has plenty of nice stores, where you can get things cheap."

"Well, I will agree to that. That's all you think about, Bubbles?"

"And like you don't think 'bout that too, Miss Melody."

" Me not going to bother Miss Nel to buy me plenty things. She send plenty for us and that is okay for now." Melody was always the most considerate and understanding of the sisters.

As they converse in their heavy Jamaican accent, one of the flight attendants, while making her rounds, stops by them and smiles. "Your first time here? Welcome." Her accent is a deep, kind of southern drawl and her smile is really welcoming. She makes the girls feel welcomed.

The captain announces that they would be landing in another ten minutes. The British Airways jet slowly descends and lands safely at the John F. Kennedy Airport. All the passengers, in appreciation of the captain's safe and accomplished mission, give a resounding applause as the aircraft taxies toward the gate.

Melody and Bubbles join in the applause, happy that they have reached America safely. They squeeze each other's hand and say, "Thank you, Jesus."

Assisted by one of the attendants, the girls clear immigration and proceed to customs where all goes smoothly. As they exit from the customs area and walk down the red carpeted walkway, they hear a voice calling, "Bubs! Mel!"

They turn to see their mother wearing a big smile. On the way home to Brooklyn, the talking does not cease until the car pulls up in front of the house on Prospect Street.

From the moment the girls arrived, the Pennycook's house was never the same again. Anel is more than happy. She is ecstatic that she is reunited with her two beautiful daughters.

Facing the Challenge

School opens on September 5th, one day after Labor Day. Melody is a bit nervous, although she tries very hard to disguise her anxiety. She feels a knot in her stomach and shivers as she puts on her opaque navy blue stockings. Stumbling from the unbalanced support of one leg, she quickly tries to break her fall by resting one hand on the edge of the bed to steady her tall, slim body.

"Calm down, Mel! Take it easy on yuhself. No, it's not a war yuh going to. It's just school with normal children like yuhself. Don't believe they will hurt, you know." She gives a wide grin, as she ends her soliloquy.

Anel, her mother, walks into the room, as Melody ends the monologue. "Is who you talking to, Melly? Hurry up before yuh late for school on your first day."

"I am ready, Mama. I wasn't talking to anybody, mam."

Melody picks up the black book bag her mother had bought for her at the Stern's summer clearance sale and heads for the kitchen. Its only contents are a five-subject notebook and the Webster dictionary she brought with her from Jamaica.

Bubbles and Roderick, their younger brother, are already at the table eating the pancakes their mother has prepared. Melody has taken a liking to the pancakes since the first time she tasted them, sometime after her arrival in Brooklyn, early summer.

"Mama is what this call? It kinda taste like fried dumpling, but only thing, it sweet," she had asked with curiosity.

"Oh! This is Aunt Jemima pancakes, served with syrup, darling," her mother had replied. "You like it?"

"Yes, Mama. Where does Aunt Jemima live? Did she bring them over or did you pick them up from her yard?" Melody had asked, innocently.

Her mother had turned from the stove, as she flipped over the last pancake in the skillet, and smiled. "No, darling. She did not bring it over. I picked it up, the mix I mean, at Foodtown, when I went shopping last Saturday."

She had held up the box of pancake mix and shown it to her daughter.

"Well, Mama, you live and learn. All I know is, I love these sweet dumplings."

Mrs. Pennycook was pleased that Melody had made the first adjustment to her new lifestyle in America. Being aware of this, she decided she would cook a variety of things for breakfast each day. She is relieved that she won't have to prepare fried dumpling and salt fish or callaloo all the time, especially since the callaloo is in a can. She won't have to cook cornmeal porridge either, although she knows the girls loved and ate this kind of food back in Jamaica. Although she likes the Jamaican breakfast edibles herself, the preparation of American breakfasts is surely simpler.

When she again went grocery shopping, she had considered picking up some Jamaican food items, but resisted. "Lawkes, man, me know seh them like this kind of food but mi can't cook this every day, so me glad seh dem seem to like the American food. Well, at least Mel love pancake." Mrs. Pennycook amused herself while shopping.

Mrs. Pennycook watches her children enjoy their breakfast and she is happy to have them all together. Yet, she is well aware of Melody's apprehension about going to school in America and truly sympathizes with her. She is cognizant of the differences between the school systems in America and Jamaica, especially in Brooklyn, where she has been living for the past ten years. She remembers coming to Brooklyn from Jamaica and living with her half-sister, Pansy, who had been living in America for over twenty years. Pansy relocated from Birmingham, England, met and married a Hispanic, and had two children. Mrs. Pennycook saw and learned a lot about school life from her niece, Delraya, who was born and bred in Brooklyn. She saw the way Delraya dressed for school and had met her friends when they came over to the house. She also had the opportunity to be educated about the school happenings by her niece the many times they sat and talked together. Anel Marks (Mrs. Pennycook -- she wasn't married then) had come to New York three weeks before the summer school break. She was exhausted the morning following her arrival because she had stayed up late talking with Pansy, her only sister. That morning, she had seen Delraya leaving the house dressed in a pair of shorts and a low cut blouse with puff sleeves. Still sleepy and drowsy, she thought for sure that her niece had a day off from school, since it was Friday, and was going shopping or somewhere else. It only dawned on Anel that Delraya had been to school, when she came home at 3:00 p.m., dropped her books on the kitchen table and gave a big sigh.

"Hi, Aunt Nel. Wish I was the lucky one at home today, rather than being in that crazy, boring school. Gaalee what a day!" Delraya had exclaimed.

"You went to school, today?"

"Yes, sure did. Why?"

"Dressed like that! Don't you wear a uniform?"

"P-e-l-e-e-a-z-e, Aunt A-n-e-l. Uniform! I do not go to a nun school."

For the days, weeks and months that followed, Anel saw more and more of the fashions her niece wore to school. She had many conversations with her sister Pansy on the subject and promised herself that she would not subject her children to this culture.

"No, sah. Me don't like this style at all. God will help me to send them to private school. I just believe a uniformed attire creates a uniformed mind. Ah mean to say, how can you tell the school children from the general public, when everybody wearing the same thing, eeh sah?"

Pansy was getting ready to watch her favorite television soap opera. "Anel, don't worry yuhself over this now, for you don't even have any children here. You will adjust when the time comes." Pansy looked at the kitchen clock, saw it was time for "All My Children," and was anxious to end the conversation. "Turn on the TV for me please, Nel," she said to her sister.

Anel had turned the television knob, as she continued to shake her head in discontent while muttering to herself. "No, sah, not me, America not going to frighten me. Right is right and principle is principle. No sah, not me atall!"

Now that her own girls were here, Anel realized that it was not possible to put them in private schools. Economically, not possible. But she was resolved to govern them the best way she could and guide them in the choice of suitable clothes for school.

* * * * * *

Melody puts the last piece of pancake in her mouth and tries to calm her reservations about going to school. During the summer, she had asked her brother Roderick (who was already attending Public School) a million questions about school. Roderick is seven years old and American-born; he is entering the second grade.

Melody has been assigned to the Eighth grade. This makes her very happy because she knows that she could have been placed in the Seventh grade. Many Jamaicans who transfer to the American school system are sometimes put back a grade for various reasons, but Melody's grades at Chenrt were excellent. Her sister Bubbles will be entering Ninth grade at the High School, which is a bit further away from home.

The Junior High School is only four blocks away, and within walking distance from their home. Melody had walked by the building many times during the summer and sometimes had stopped for a while just to stare at the brown concrete building. Boys were always playing basketball in the area she assumed was the playground. She was not too excited about the school's appearance.

"Boy, this reminds me of some prison ground," she thought, the first time she had seen the school.

Melody remembers clearly that, in Jamaica, even if the school building was not in tip top shape, needed a face lift of paint or needed to have a few windows repaired, the school's environment appeared inviting. She is cognizant that school is a place away from home, that practices strict rules and discipline and administers corporal punishment when the need arises. Nevertheless, she had enjoyed attending school, where she had a lot of fun with her friends, especially her two close friends, Lorna Stone and Retinella Roper.

Each time she had passed by her new school, she envisioned her old school grounds -- the playing field at Chenrt was bigger with no concrete areas, except at the very front of the building. There were lots of trees, and the hedges were bordered with red and yellow Hibiscus flowers which seemed to relax in the bright sunshine and smile at all the children passing by. Sometimes the students were startled by an approaching bee and would twist and turn their heads and flap their hands in an attempt to chase it away. If the bee lingered around a child, the other students would yell, "Don't box him weh man! Is money yu gwine get." This was an old superstition they had heard and believed.

Melody can almost taste the large common 'hairy' mangoes that grew on the tree which hung almost fully over the far end of the playing field, behind her classroom in Jamaica. The mango tree belonged to the Porters, whose property was next to Chenrt Town All Age School, but during mango season, the mangoes were common property, shared by all who passed by.

After standing in front of the school, the memories running wild, Melody would slowly walk away with a sigh, saying, "Ah well, me here already!" At other times, her thoughts would be interrupted by a kid on a bike bearing down upon her at full speed on the sidewalk; she would jump onto the curb for safety.

* * * * * *

After breakfast, the three children put on their lightweight windbreaker jackets, purchased at the Labor Day sale at Sears, as they prepare to leave for school. Mrs. Pennycook gives them a motherly kiss on their cheeks and bids them goodbye. She, too, is a bit nervous and prays a silent prayer for God to guide, and protect her children. She is especially concerned about her two daughters who are about to make a cultural adjustment to the American school system. "Just remember to run from trouble if you see it coming . . . be good," she calls out to them, as they leave.

She waves the last goodbye as the children descend the steps leading to the sidewalk. Bubbles has further to travel to her school, so she hurries ahead of Melody and Roderick.

Mrs. Pennycook returns to the kitchen where she makes a hot cup of Jamaican chocolate tea from the bars the girls brought with them from Jamaica. She moves about in the kitchen, distractedly, with her mind on the girls. Placing the cup on the counter, she returns to the sidewalk to catch a last glimpse of her three children. But she is too late, they are already out of her view.

She slowly walks back to the kitchen and sits down to drink her chocolate. Realizing that it has cooled a bit, she pours it into a small pot to reheat it on the electric stove. As she does this, she hums her favorite song, "*Jesus Savior pilot me, over life's tempestuous sea,*" then repeats the first line, again changing "pilot me" to "pilot them." She pours the reheated chocolate into her cup and, as she sips it slowly, her thoughts wander to the school grounds and focuses on Melody. She is mostly worried about Melody and is not sure why. Or, maybe she *does* know but is afraid to admit it -- yes, Melody is special to her. Mrs. Pennycook's mind wanders to the day Melody was born and lingers on the time she spent nurturing her before putting her in Grannyma's custody.

Her thoughts are interrupted by a ringing sound. At first, she is not sure if it is the doorbell or the telephone. Realizing, after several rings, that it is the telephone, she reaches for the yellow receiver hanging on the kitchen wall.

"Hello."

It is her husband, Winston. "Yes Win, the children are gone me dear, and I am just here thinking about the girls, especially you know who! See you later, nuh."

She hangs up the phone and finishes her chocolate tea. She is determined to clean up the kitchen and take her nap before leaving for the 3:00 p.m. to 11:00 p.m. shift at the City Hospital where she is employed as a licensed practical nurse.

* * * * * *

Melody and Roderick continue their walk to their respective schools, after Bubbles separated from them. They are both early. Melody stands by the fence of her brother's school (the Junior High is only half a block around the corner on the next street), and passes the time talking quietly. Roderick points out some of his friends to his sister, but Melody's eyes are canvassing the grounds of the Elementary School. She is experiencing a new culture. It is definitely not like Jamaica!

The September morning air is still cool. Some of the mothers who have accompanied their children to school are wearing faded blue jeans and dirty white sneakers. Others are wearing house slippers with Fall coats, disguising the house dresses they refuse to take off, to escort their children to the school. They stand inside and outside of the schoolyard in clusters, unattractively dressed. Some wear large pink, blue and aqua hair rollers in their hair covered by headscarves; others display the hair rollers for all to see.

Melody is both amused and cynical. Mothers of kindergartners, first graders and some second graders have accompanied their children to school on the first day. Screaming kindergartners are bellowing at the top of their voices, seemingly attempting to master some of the highest musical octaves. Others, with their heads buried in their mothers' coats, shyly sob as their mothers coax them with comforting words and make promises that they themselves know they cannot keep. "If you stop crying honey, I'll buy you that new bike tomorrow." Or "I will take you skating."

The teachers watch and listen to the wailing five- and six-year- olds and look in disdain at the mothers who unknowingly encourage the children in their tantrums. It is obvious that the more they pity the child the louder the crying gets. Once in a while, an uncontrollable child goes into hysterics while the mother hugs him, embarrassed by the scene the child is making. Melody hears the remarks of a teacher as she passes her. "I see this every year. Don't they know that the more they pamper, the more vulnerable the child becomes?" "I wish they would say goodbye and leave," says the teacher cynically.

The wailing children eventually leave their mothers' sides, while still crying; when the teachers beckon for the mothers to leave. Melody speculates that in the classrooms, the teachers have boxes of tissues ready to dry the tears, and the snotty noses.

Satisfied that she has seen enough, Melody waves goodbye to her brother and heads around the block to her school. "See you later, Roderick, and remember to wait right here for me this evening ," she reminds him.

Melody joins the line with the eighth graders. She was told exactly what to do when she registered in August. The multi-cultural line of about twenty-eight boys and girls with book-bags propped over their shoulders slowly move into the building to climb the stairwell to the second floor. Melody looks ahead of her at all the children in front and gives a quick glance over her shoulders at those behind and around her.

"Me neva see so much different race of people in one place yet," she remarks to herself.

She thinks of the diversity of people in Jamaica: Chinese, Indians and some whites, but the majority are Blacks. But the cross-section of children she sees around her now appear to be more diverse. She has difficulty pinpointing the various nationalities, but it is quite clear that the school houses many different races. Melody can only positively identify the Whites, Blacks and Spanish, particularly the Puerto Ricans. She immediately remembers the song and repeats the first line. "God Bless America"

A girl in front of her (Melody assumes she is Spanish because of her accent) is ascending the stairs and Melody cannot help but notice the clothes she is wearing.

"Mi Jesus, help me. Lawd, a wha' dat she wearing. This no right atall! How can the government make school children wear these kind of clothes to school? Shorts! And feh har more than short. It really sho-o-rt."

Melody shakes her head in disgust and heads towards her classroom, Room 453, as her mind strays again back to Jamaica. In Jamaica, all school children wear a special uniform to school, no matter how small the school. At Chenrt Town All Age, Melody did not like the color of her uniform (brown plaid tunic with dark brown short sleeves blouse) but she had to wear it anyway. That was the rule, and all students abided by it. She grins as she recalls the time she showed up for school without a uniform back in Jamaica.

* * * * * *

She was about nine years old and it was the first day of school for the New Year. Her grandmother did not want to keep Bubbles and Melody out of school just because they did not have their new uniforms. Their mother was late in sending the money from America to buy the material for the uniforms to be made by Miss Clarice, the dressmaker. At least, that was what Grannyma thought: that the money order was posted late – until she received a call on New Year's Day from their mother, Anel.

Grannyma had just removed the tin pan from the head of the big brown fowl which she had just butchered for the New Year's Day dinner. As she wiped away the speck of blood that flew from the fowl's severed head to her face, she heard a knocking at the iron gate. She looked up and saw Gladstone, the next-door neighbor's son.

"Granniema, you have phone call from 'Merica, mam," Gladstone called out to her, his voice cracking as a result of puberty.

She quickly washed her feathery, bloody hands, wiped them in the old skirt apron tied around her waist and ran next door to get the phone. She knew it was her daughter Anel calling. As she hastened to get the long distance call, she hoped for the day when she would have her own phone which her daughter had promised her.

"But then again, even if Nel send the money to install the phone, no telling when the Telephone Company will get to it," Grannyma tells herself, as she waits for the connection. It is indeed a well-known fact that getting a phone in Jamaica can be an endless wait sometimes.

"Hello Nel dear, Happy New Year mi child. How you doing, everything all right, how the weather it cold, nuh?" She did not pause, as she was so delighted to hear from her daughter.

"Yes, Mama, I am fine, Happy New Year to you too, and the girls.

And it is very cold, twenty degrees today, mam. I am not staying long, just want to hear your voice and find out if you get the money order yet."

"Not yet, I was wondering how you mail it so late this time, it not going to come in time to buy the uniform for the girls. Don't know what ah going to do, but we will see, don't worry youself."

"You didn't get it yet! That's strange. I mailed it from the first of December. Is the Christmas mail, you nuh. Please write and tell me when you get it. I just hope them didn't steal it. Take care, Mama, bye."

By the end of the week, the money came but it was too late to get the uniforms in time for school. So, on the first day of school, Melody and Bubbles were dressed in one of their Sunday School outfits.

Melody walked into her classroom that Monday morning and was stopped by her teacher, Miss Goodhall.

"And where you going dress up in pretty frock today, little Miss? Today is not Sunday, you know. It is Monday, and you come to learn, not to show off. Eh! eh!" She placed her hands akimbo.

"Miss" (this was how students addressed teachers in Jamaica), ah don't come to show off, Mam. Mi uniform wasn't ready for school and mi grandmother didn't want me to miss school the first day."

"Are you sure Miss . . . (Miss Goodhall wasn't sure of Melody's last name, since this was a new class, so she glanced at her roll book), Miss . . . Miss . . . ," she repeated, as she scanned the forty or so names.

"Melody Marks." (This was her family name before she was fully adopted by her step-father and her surname changed to Pennycook).

"Yes, I see it here, Melody Marks. I want you to go down to the Principal's office and tell him the same story you told me and, if he gives you the okay to stay in school, you can come right back. I still believe seh yuh get yuh pretty dress for Christmas from America and want to come show off."

Melody looked at the teacher, whose eyeglasses rested on her nose that barely had a bridge to hold them. She rolled her eyes upward showing the cornea and thought in her heart that Miss Goodhall grudged her and was jealous of her nice dress, which came from America.

"Red eye," Melody grumbled, hissing her teeth as she walked away from the classroom.

She went down to the principal's office and explained the situation and all she had to do was bring in a note from her grandmother the next day.

* * * * * *

This was how school was run in Jamaica. Whenever a student was out of uniform, a proper explanation had to be given. She was not too excited when her mother told her she did not have to wear a uniform to school in America, but there was nothing she could do about it. This too is another adjustment she had to get used to and overcome.

When Melody's flashback ended, the Spanish girl, who Melody thought was not dressed appropriately for school, had long vanished down the hallway. As she takes her seat in the classroom, her mind still lingers on Jamaica -- but any further recollections are halted by a loud voice over the school's Public Address System. It is the Principal, Mr. Powers, announcing 'Home Room time.' Melody is on the alert for this one. Her cousin Delraya, had clued her in on this ritual during the summer. This was routine activity in the public school system in America, Delraya had said.

"Unoo don't say prayers over here?" she had asked her cousin, with surprise.

Home room time, she told Melody, starts the school day officially, but rather than singing a religious song and saying a selected school prayer, the pledge of allegiance to the flag of the United States is said. Melody then had shared with her cousin, the devotional exercises most schools practiced in Jamaica.

"My favorite song was Immortal Invisible," she told Delraya, and began to sing it.

After she finished the song that day, Delraya gave her a big applause and commented on her beautiful voice. "You go cousin. You got potentials," but she continued to defend the school culture.

"Well, it is almost the same thang, just that we ain't sing no songs and say no prayers."

Delraya had tried to convince her, but Melody had argued with her and, in a matter of fact way, she made her understand that it should not be remotely compared to the Jamaican way. "Totally different," she had emphasized. During that conversation, she also learned that prayer was not permitted in the schools in America. In her follow up research at the library, she learned that this was a result of the efforts of one Madeline O'Hare who had successfully campaigned to ban this practice of prayer in schools some years ago, under the guise of the *Separation of Church and State*.

    The Eighth Grade class of twenty-eight students rise to their feet. Placing their right hands on their heart, they face the large red, white and blue flag which hangs from the green-board. The teacher, Mrs. Varma, also stands with her right hand placed on her heart, as she eyes the class to make sure everyone is standing. Melody does as her classmates do, and tries to say the words from memory without looking at the piece of paper she had written the pledge on, when Roderick recited it to her. She had studied the words and knows them quite well and is glad she did. She does not want to appear too odd on her first day. She hopes that by blending in, no one will detect that she is a newcomer to the school. She only stumbles over a few words, because she cannot keep up with the pace and the American pronunciations. A Puerto Rican girl glances at her and smiles and Melody returns a quick, shy smile and lowers her voice as she continues saying the pledge.

    "I pledge allegiance to the Flag of the United States of America and to the Republic for which it Stands, One Nation under God, Indivisible, with Liberty and Justice For All."

    There is a rustle of movement and chatter as the students sit down after the pledge. As Melody sits, she looks scornfully at her desk. "Lawkes, this desk mark up mark up, eeh! Is what this, 'S-t-a-c-i-e loves Jay-t-a-h.' Ah wha kind a name this?" She gives a smirky smile as she tries to decipher the carved-out inscription that is written on her desk. It shows a heart-shaped drawing with an arrow going through it. She looks up as Mrs. Varma clears her throat and begins taking attendance.

    "Natasha Albright, Waukesha Anderson . . . ."

    "Eh! seems like everybody name some different kind a 'Sha' in America."

    Melody listens and watches all the responses of the students to the roll call. Most of the students only raise their hands without looking at Mrs. Varma and barely answer to their names. Some are engaged in conversation with a friend, while others are distracted by some other means.

    "Melody Pennycook."

    "Here, Miss," she blurts out, quickly, as she hears her name.

    A few heads turn and look at her and a hushed burst of laughter follows.

"Is wha dem ah laugh fah? Is so we answer to we names in Jamaica and is so me answer to my name in America." Melody blushes a little and is somewhat embarrassed.

"Well, class, welcome back to school. I hope y'all had a great summer. From your class schedule, you should know where all your classes are. And, yep! First period English is with me. So in order to know a little about you, your in-class assignment for the next twenty minutes is to write an essay on 'The One Thing I Enjoyed Most This Summer.' And tell me a little about yourself."

Melody takes out her notebook and begins to write. English and Spanish are her favorite subjects. She takes the opportunity also, to glance at her class schedule and notices that she has seven other classes that she has to travel to, and she is a bit apprehensive. She wonders if she will find her way around the building. She already knows the gym and cafeteria room by their marked décor, when she visited the school the first time.

Back in Chenrt All Age in Jamaica, students stayed in one class for most of their subjects, except for Biology and Physical Education (PE). The teachers there usually traveled to the classes in the lower grades. At grade 10 and higher, students traveled to classes.

Melody writes the title on the page, her name and the date and begins to write her essay: *"My name is Melody Patrice Pennycook. I am five feet eight inches tall, although I am only thirteen years old. Yes, I know I am very tall for my age, but I have been this tall since I was eleven years old"*.

She gives a timid smile as she remembers how she was teased by many and was often called "longulala" which in Jamaican dialect means "very tall".

She continues her essay: *"My eyes are brown and I weigh . . . , well, I think I'll pass on this one. Anyway, I have one brother and one sister, at least that I know of."*

Melody is aware that there is a strong possibility that she may have other siblings. Her Dad is a foreigner and is or was probably married and has other children. She has friends who are one of many children fathered by one man but have different mothers. For example, her best friend, Retinella knows all her fourteen brothers and sisters, yet she is the only child for her mother, Miss Ruby Gentles. Melody continues her essay:

I was born in Kingston, but was raised in Spanish Town, Jamaica,

West Indies. I lived with my grandmother until June of this year when I migrated to America to live with my mother and step-father. I really liked going to school at least when I lived back in Jamaica; now I am not sure if I still do because I am new to my surroundings.

She then starts a new paragraph to talk about what she enjoyed:

The most important thing I enjoyed this Summer, was Summer in America (well, to say the least, since I spent all Summer thinking about my new school). I arrived in June, and I am not sure if I really enjoyed anything special, because, all the time, I kept thinking about going to school in America. However, I must be honest and say, overall, coming to America was exciting and adventurous. I always dreamed about this great country I heard about and had seen on television. I guess I can say that coming to see and finally live with my Mom was an enjoyable thing for me.

Melody writes two full pages mentioning all the other things she did for the Summer and is finished just before the bell rings for the second period. She reads over her essay quickly and makes corrections where applicable but she has second thoughts after reading it. She believes she was too candid in her expression about some of her experiences in America, up to the present time. At thirteen years old, Melody can be considered a good writer. And although she knows she applied diplomacy where necessary, she feels she could have been less candid. She consoles herself that she could have spelt it out even more vividly. As she hands in her essay, she wonders about the impression it will make on her teacher.

"I hope Miss don't think seh me too ' bright'. If me really should write how me really feel, eh! eh! Dem would send me back to me yard."

The things she did not write about whirl around in her head. Even now, they are at the forefront of her mind: She did not write about how disappointed she was when she first arrived in Brooklyn, her new home and community. She did not like the way the houses are built closely together, with some joining together, and projecting out on the sidewalk. Some are so close, that you could actually step off the curb up into your living room. There are no big backyards in the section of Brooklyn where she lives, and if there are any backyards at all, they are small and joined to the neighbor's yard. If the truth was told, she was truly taken aback by her new surroundings. However, she enjoyed what she experienced at the airport (and that was an experience in and of itself): The mere vastness of the airport had been fascinating to both Bubbles and herself. She smiles as she remembers how excited she had been.

"Mi know sey anybody could tell seh mi just come up feh the first time when dem hear me asking if over there so is airport too? Lawkes, Melody, you neva did haffe act so frighten and fool-fool."

Melody looks at her schedule one more time to verify her room number for her second period class. Second period is History. While canvassing the doors for the right class, the Puerto Rican girl who sat beside her in Home Room catches up with her.

"Hi, my name is Ariel. Ariel Granada. Sem like you are new here, no! Mi here second time, I show you room."

"Sure, thanks, and, yes, I am new here in this school and this country. My name is Melody Pennycook; you can call me Mel."

Both girls talk as they walk to the class.

"You from Jamaika, no! The island, si? Mi from island too, Puerto Rico."

At first, Melody did not know what country Ariel was talking about, but when she said, island, she realized she was referring to Jamaica.

"Yes, the island in the sun, they say. How do you know where I am from? You been to Jamaica before?" Melody then gives a wide grin because she knows it was her accent that gave her away.

Melody and Ariel take seats next to each other , as the bell rings to begin second period. The History teacher is a tall white man, with lots of beard, like Santa Claus, sideburns and a receding hairline.

"Okay, let's all settle down now," he says. He turns to the board and writes his name on the top left hand side . . . Mr. John Brandis. He then quickly takes attendance, explains the syllabus for the school year, then hands out the textbook. "This is your history book which should be wrapped neatly and your names written on the covers only. If you should lose this book, you will pay for it."

The textbook is called *American Heritage--Volume 2*.

After he is sure that all the students have a book, Mr. Brandis begins the first lesson, *The American Civil War*. Melody is intrigued with the first ten minutes of the lesson. She thinks back to what she learned about the English Invasion of 1655 at Chenrt. In that war, the British won the war against Spain, after which Jamaica was ruled by the British. By being able to compare and identify the similarities between what she learnt at Chenrt and what she is currently learning about American history,

Melody has a better understanding of the subject. She tries to keep up with all the names and places and the different states that were involved in the Civil War.

It is a lot to take in, but she has to adjust now that she is in America. She has to study its history. She thinks of the well-known cliche and modifies it: "Yes, 'when in Rome, you have to do as the Romans do.'"

By the end of the class, Melody has taken a page of notes. She makes a point of copying the homework assignment from the board. She has always been a dedicated student and does not see failure in her future.

"I am not the least worried, no sah! If me need help, mi cousin Delraya will help me. She is American."

All her other classes are exciting and challenging. Introduction to Spanish, Social Studies, Mathematics, General Science, Gym and Lunch make up the eight periods for the day. Math was and still is her least favorite subject, but she is determined to at least make an above average grade.

She sits in the third seat from the front in Math and grins as she listens intently to Mr. Shakaal, the Math teacher. "Bwoy, it seems like seh is mostly man teachers dem have, fe Math and Science subjects, (her Science teacher is also a man, but he is white).

Shak . . . Shakaal! Americans have funny names, sah!"

Mr. Shakaal is an African American. His attire, a long tent-like robe and a small hat, indicate to Melody that he is in some kind of movement. "Same way some of the real Rastafarians dress up back home, only thing is, him don't have any dreadlocks."

Fourth period is lunch and although it is not a classroom environment per se, it is just as disciplined as in the classroom. There is an assigned teacher on duty in the cafeteria and, since it is the first day of school, assigned seats are given.

Her Gym teacher is a young lady. Melody is not sure of her race, but she looks white. She is not too impressed with her first gym experience and, in fact, places it as one of her least favorite subjects. Melody was never very athletic but she enjoyed her Physical Education (PE) classes in Jamaica. One of the popular PE game activities was netball and it was played on the netball court on the playing field. Netball was a professional girls sport, while football was for the boys.

At 2:45 p.m., Melody finishes her first day at school in, Junior High and walks down the wide brownstone steps to meet her brother. She had made it through her first day and hopes she will survive the remaining three days. The Labor Day holiday had shortened the week, which was considered a blessing in disguise by Melody.

By the end of the four-day school week, she is positive that she has learnt a lot but is smart enough to know, this is only the beginning.

* * * * * *

"Come on, Melody, why you is walking so fast?" asks Roderick, trying to keep up with his sister's pace.

Melody is shivering from the morning's coolness, as she walks to school. September had been much warmer. It is now October First and it appears that Indian Summer is finally over. Now, it was beginning to feel really like Fall. She folds her arms around her chest and makes big strides to get to the schoolyard.

"You are. Not you is," she corrects Roderick, looking at him with stupefaction, making a face, and rolling her semi-hazel eyes upwards, revealing a portion of the cornea.

She hates when he uses bad grammar. She also had overheard other children speak that way. She cannot understand why it is so difficult to use proper grammar. Once when she had heard a little girl say, "Yes am is," she had shaken her head in pity and smiled. "Me might talk patois (Jamaican dialect) and sound funny to them, but when it comes to proper grammar I can speak it.

"You not cold? Well I am!" she responds to Roderick's question.

She slows down, realizing that when she gets to school, she still has to stand in the cold until the bell rings. "Be ready Rod, and I won't wait if you are playing with your friends," Melody warns her brother.

"I'll be ready," Roderick responds grudgingly.

He is happy to have his older sister around, but already he loathes her bossy attitude. Melody arrives at school, and sees her friend Ariel. They have become very good friends over the past weeks. In the evenings and on weekends, they talk on the phone, endlessly, when they are done with homework and chores.

"Owoo, Owoo, muy frio, today, Melody!" Ariel's teeth are chattering as she walks towards Melody.

Melody smiles at the way Ariel speaks in Spanish and English at the same time. "Yes, it is kinda cold, today. Si, muy frio," she teases.

While they talk about their weekend activities, the bell rings for the class line-up. Melody looks around her as she stands in line. "It look like more children come to school this week?" she comments.

She is correct; the lines are longer. She notices a very handsome boy who looks different from the others she had seen previously. She doesn't recall seeing him before and wonders if he is Jamaican or American.

Ariel notices her interest and nudges her on the elbow. "He cute, no!" she says, with a wry smile, in her Spanish accent.

Both girls giggle as they walk to their home-room. Just before Mrs. Varma calls the class to attention, and the pledge is said, the boy they noticed outside walks into the room. Melody feels butterflies in her stomach and blushes as he hands Ms. Varma a slip of paper. He is gestured to his seat in a hurry by Ms. Varma, to the left rear of the class. It is two seats away from Melody's seat. Her heart tingles the more and she quietly scolds herself. "No badda wid that, Miss Melody, calm yuhself down. You know you are not that boy crazy . . . but it is something about him different, you must admit."

She places her right hand across her chest as she joins in the saying of the Pledge of Allegiance to the Flag, which she now does fluently. Occasionally, she peeps at the new boy who has his hands on his chest but is not saying anything. After the pledge is done, Ms. Varma takes attendance and Melody learns the new boy's name is Kirk Kensington, and his accent is different. British.

"Me know, man!" Melody snaps with elation. "Me know seh him not American."

She glances at Ariel and gives an "excuse me smile," as she bites her lips firmly and lowers her chin.

The next day in the class line-up, Melody learns that Kirk was born in Sheffield, England but his parents are Jamaicans. He lived in Canada for two years and recently moved to America.

"I am from Jamaica too, you know. Where in Jamaica your parents came from?" she asks him excitedly.

Melody is making conversation, and trying to sound proper. She is happy that Kirk has her roots.

"Me Mom is from St. Thomas and me Dad from Portland, but they've been in England for a long time. And I've got me some older brothers and sisters and we all were born in England, actually."

She is intrigued by his accent. Melody is convinced that they will be friends, good friends, even with no sentiments attached; still, he is a boy. She has always cautioned herself not to be boy crazy, but she really likes him and she has not felt the same way with the other boys so far. It is still too early to tell if she will be really close friends, with any American boy. Melody has already discovered some clash or barrier in her feelings towards American boys. Some are real cute and handsome, but there is something that stops her from going crazy over them. She just cannot figure it out exactly and it bothers her a bit.

Trouble Is Coming

It is Friday, the last day of school for another week. Melody, Ariel and Kirk are having lunch together in the cafeteria. The three have become good buddies, with their Caribbean background as a common bond. Melody still feels butterflies when she is around Kirk, especially when he speaks. It is apparent that there is a mutual feeling between them but Kirk is a bit shy and controls himself.

Kirk recognizes that Melody is indeed beautiful -- a different kind of Jamaican girl. Different from those he saw when he visited Jamaica and those he met in Canada. He marvels at her complexion, the length and texture of her hair and how she looks. She reminds him of the mixed-marriage English kids. But he dares not meddle and ask personal questions. He does not know her that well. Melody, on the other hand, likes his mature attitude, although he only turned fourteen recently.

As they stand on line to get their lunch, the three chat about different things. Melody is more loquacious than her friends.

"I don't know when I will ever get to love this kinda food," she remarks in the American accent she sometimes uses. She has learned to modify her speech when she speaks to her school friends and in public, but her pronounced Jamaican accent is still detectable, especially when she is home or among fellow Jamaican friends. She is determined to cherish the language, no matter what, even if she eventually manages the American accent well. She recalls that in Jamaica, the American accent was called a "twang". Her friends are amused by her flexibility in switching back and forth from the patois (which they now understand) to the American accent. "Man! Jamaican lunch was sweeter than this. We had the regular school lunch delivered called 'Bolo Slush,' and sometimes it was really nice."

She explains how the lunch was delivered hot, in aluminum-insulated containers, by vans, to the primary schools. "Schools just like this, not the high schools," she reminisces. "Yes man, it came about 11:30 a.m., and we made up a song about the lunch van."

She gives a wide grin and begins to sing quietly to avoid being heard by the other students. "One, two, three, four, bolo man a come." Her friends stare at her with elation as she captures their attention.

"Sometimes the food didn't look too good, it looked like slush. That is why we made up the song. But most times, it tasted very good and we got our bellyful."

The line moves closer and closer to the serving window as she continues to relate the good old lunch time tales to her two friends. Bolo slush, she explains, was only one aspect of the school lunch in Jamaica. Lunch could also be bought from food vendors outside or on the school premises.

"Yes man! We could buy hot patties and coco bread, and chocolate cremo milk from the shop or from anybody selling lunch. But my favorite was bag." She closes her eyes in an effort to recall the memories, and licks her lips.

"Bag!" Ariel and Kirk ask in unison. "What is that?"

"Bag, my friends, was a brown paper bag, just like the ones you put a sandwich in and take to work or school. However, this bag contained three to four small golden brown, fried dumplings, and a piece of fried salt fish. It was delicious and, the bag was so greasy, you could see the dumplings through the bag."

Ariel and Kirk now understand what she is talking about. Melody's description causes Kurt to drool. He loves fried dumplings and enjoys them when his mother prepares them at home. He is embarrassed by his drool, and turns away from Melody and Ariel as he wipes his mouth with the back of his hand.

Melody ends that part of her story, by telling them how she drank snowball (shaved ice with flavored syrup) afterwards to "wash down" the dumplings. She is eager to continue her lunch tale, but they are now at the cafeteria's serving window where they have a choice of hamburger or hot dogs with French fries and a pickle (small tangy cucumber soaked in vinegar) on the side. After making their selections, they sit at a table in the back of the cafeteria.

"So where was I? Yes, yes, that was only the food part I told you about. Wait until I tell you about the snacks," Melody says, as she takes a bite out of her hot dog and chews for a second before resuming her lunch tale. "We had a lot of snacks and sweetie (candy) to choose from. And me loved them all, and use to buy them at lunch and recess time." She sticks some fries into her mouth and chews again. "We ate *bustamante* -- some call it *stagga back* -- *asham, drops and grater cake*, and whole heap more."

Of course, each time she mentions something that is not familiar, she describes it for her friends. "Well, stagga back is like toffee, but very, very hard, and it is black. It is so hard to bite, that as you hold it and try to bite it you stumble backwards (stagger back -- loosing your balance). Asham is a parched corn, grounded to powder (grayish color) with sugar added. You dust it on your tongue and eat it. Drops and grater cake are made out of coconut and they are loaded with sugar. Drops is dark in color and grater cake is white or white and pink coloring. And I must tell you about the fruits, too. Ymm. . mmm! My favorites are mangoes, guinep and june plum, to this day. Only hope I can find them in America."

Ariel's eyes beam in response, as she recognizes the fruits Melody mentions. "Si, my country, tambien. We gat all these fruits and yes I love mangoes -- delicioso."

"Maybe I will get used to American food one day," says Melody, as lunch period comes to a close. "This lunch was good for a change today."

But Melody is a bit uneasy. When they had first sat down for lunch, she had noticed three girls sitting at the table in front of them. They appeared to be between the ages of twelve to fourteen years. She had seen them around the school before. These girls had also been on the lunch line in front of Melody and her friends. She had noticed that as she talked to Ariel and Kirk, they looked back at her, intermittently, talking, and giggling. Now, each time she raised her head from her plate, it was obvious that the girls' attention was focused on them.

The three girls whisper and giggle each time Melody's eyes meet theirs. She tries to ignore them.

"What time is it Kirk?" she asks. "I need to go to my locker for my sneakers. Should have worn them from this morning."

Her next class is gym and although she has her gym shorts on under her jumper dress, she had worn her ankle length boots to school since it was very cold in the morning. Melody picks up her book bag and heads toward the door so that she can be the first one out. She reaches the middle of the cafeteria and turns around to speak to her friends.

"See you later in gym," she calls out to Ariel."

She then turns around to leave the cafeteria, only to collide with one of the girls who had been sitting across from her.

"Oops! Excuse me, I am sorry," Melody apologizes.

The girl stands close, with her face almost touching Melody's nose. Her lips are set in a pout and her breathing is fast, as if she is out of breath.

"You iz Jemaikan?"

Melody is surprised at the girl's response. She smells trouble.

"Yes, why?" she responds.

"Thought so, just wanna make sure. Hmm . . . mmm, a oreo cookie. And a Jemaikan. Well, Miss salt and pepper, you better watch where you going next time."

The girl walks towards her two friends and they all laugh. Kirk and Ariel try to catch up to Melody, but she is already out the door and heading to her locker. In five minutes, the bell rings for the start of the next period.

"What was that all about, Melody? Do you know that girle?" Ariel is curious when both girls meet in the Gym and partner for basketball.

Why did the girl ask her if she is a Jamaican and what did she mean when she said oreo cookie? Melody suspects it is some kind of joke or tease, but she is not sure. She is not yet familiar with the slang and phrases in America. During gym class, she tries to focus on perfecting her basketball game, but her thoughts keep wandering back to the incident. She usually doesn't mind Gym but, today, she is extremely exhausted and just wants to go home immediately.

After Gym, Melody and Ariel walk to their lockers to put their belongings away. They bump into Kirk, as they collect their books for their next class, so they climb the stairs together and head toward the classroom.

"Cho man, I wish I was going home now," Melody says to her friends, with a yawn.

"Why is that Melody? Having a bad day, are you, now?" Kirk asks with concern.

Melody shrugs her shoulder expressing indifference to his concern, walks to her seat and sits down. Luck is on her side, for most of the class is a film presentation. She could not be happier!

"Good," she thinks, "I can just sit and look and if sleep comes, I won't stop the nod."

When the bell rings, signaling the end of the period, Melody is thrilled. She hurries out the door without saying goodbye to Kirk and Ariel, and meets Roderick at the entrance of his school. They begin their walk home in silence. Roderick notices her pensiveness, but remains talkative. He is excited about the science project on rainfall he did in class.

"Holy smokes (coining Batman and Robin), Melody, you shoulda seen my project. Sure hope I get an A."

"Good for you, Rod," she replies, disinterestedly.

"C'mon Mel, hey, what's wrong with you. You ain't too happy? Did somebody mess with you or something, today?"

"Me all right."

They are four houses away from their house, when they hear a yell from across the street. "Jemaikan oreo, get back on your boat and go back to Jemaika and get outta my way."

Melody looks across the street and sees the girl she bumped into at school at lunchtime. She pretends as if the words are not meant for her and climbs the steps behind her brother as he rings the doorbell. Their mother opens the door.

"Hi Mama," they say, in unison.

"Hi Mel! Rod!"

Melody walks sheepishly pass her mother and goes directly to her room. Usually, she would make a beeline to the kitchen to check to see if there is mail on the table: she still communicates regularly with her friend Retinella in Jamaica.

Mrs. Pennycook detects that something is wrong but decides to wait until her daughter relaxes for a while in her room before prying the truth out of her. She recalls her fear the first day Melody started school. She has always dreaded the danger and the uncertainties her half-white West Indian daughter would face in Public School in Brooklyn.

Melody's mixed birth is apparent. She does not look like the typical African American or West Indian going to an inner-city school. Her good looks and the fact that she is an immigrant from Jamaica could create a big problem. Mrs. Pennycook is wary to voice her opinions about the cause of her fears, but it is well known that Jamaicans can be singled out more than any other West Indian or Caribbean immigrants. She has heard many stories of the friction that erupts between African Americans and West Indians. She has had personal experience with this in the workplace for several years. Something about West Indians (she cannot pinpoint for sure what), creates a problem with other Black Americans. She thanks God for those good American friends she has. She is glad that no matter where you go in the world, there are always good people of whatever nationality around.

Mrs. Pennycook wants to believe that Melody will be lucky to sail through school smoothly without any problems. But she knows only time will tell. She tries hard to erase the stories she has heard from friends and relatives about the problems and the social pressures many Jamaican students face in school. However, she also cannot negate the fact that many Jamaican students also blend easily into the American mainstream.

"Everybody different, and it depends how you luck comes. It seems like some of these poor school pickney blend in easily, like Bubbles, for instance, she seems fine to me. But some have to fight to be a part of the system. Then, there is them poor misfortunate ones who just cannot fit into the system and live in pain 'til them leave school. I wonder where me Mel going to fit in?" she ponders.

Mrs. Pennycook is off from work today, so she waits until after dinner and when Melody finishes her homework to speak with her daughter. She enters the room Melody and Bubbles share, carrying a big Sears & Roebuck shopping bag.

"Mama" (many Jamaican mothers affectionately call their daughters by this term), she calls out to her daughter. "You finish your homework yet?"

"Uh huh, Mama."

"You all right, sweetheart?"

" I am all right, Mama."

"Come on, Mama, darling, you know you cannot fool your mother."
"What happened today at school?"

"Nothing, Mama," Melody begins, then pauses, "is . . . is just some girls, well one girl said something and asked if I am Jamaican."

Melody relates the full incident to her mother. Mrs. Pennycook's heartbeat accelerates and she takes a deep breath. She immediately sees that trouble is coming after her Melody. Yes, she concludes, Melody will fit into the "fight to belong or live in the pain" category until she finishes school. She senses and feels the homesickness her daughter is experiencing and offers her own encouragement.

"Don't pay them any mind, me love, and when you see her walk far from her. And remember what I told you before you started school. Stay away and out of trouble. Run from it if possible, but (she emphasized the 'but') . . . but I must also tell you, if bad come to worse, help yourself. Dem seh duppy (ghost) know who to frighten. And if you allow duppy feh scare you, you will forever be scared. So, Mel, me love, read between the lines."

As Melody looks at her mother, her fears and her homesickness subside and she feels a sense of security from her mother's word. Because of her mother's frequent visits to Jamaica, and over the few months since Melody has been living in America, they have developed a close bond. Realizing that her mother is just like Grannyma, she thinks of the phrase, "chip don't fall too far from the block."

Her mother hands her the Sears bag. In it, Melody finds a blue, wool winter coat. Mrs. Pennycook had put it on lay-a-way, so she could pay for it bit by bit before the cold weather settled in. Later, when Bubbles gets in, she too will be surprised with a new coat.

"Thanks Mama, this comes in on time, cause me freezing, already. Man it is cold," Melody says with a chuckle, already forgetting her troubles.

"Mel, you don't feel anything yet, mi child, this no cold. It gwine to get worse!"

Melody takes her new coat out of the bag, tries it on, then hangs it up in her closet. "Thanks again, Mama, for *everything*."

Her mother gives her a big hug, kisses her and leaves the room. Melody jumps out of bed, brushes her teeth, says her prayers and goes back to bed. She lays her head against her pillow, resting it in the palm of her hands, and stares at the poster with the Jamaican Coat of Arms. Soon she is fast asleep. She is really tired. It has been truly a long day, both physically and mentally.

Understanding the Difference

Two weeks before Halloween, Melody has learned a lot about this American festival from the commercials she saw on television. Houses on her block are decorated with replicas of skeletons, pumpkins with imprinted faces, large fake black bats and cobweb impressions over doors. In the front yard of one house, there is a small tombstone with the inscription R.I.P. A house next to her school, has a display of a stuffed scarecrow figure bordered by stalks of straw and other cornfield replica. Melody is more than curious; she is confused, and confirms to herself that America is different from Jamaica in many ways. Roderick had mentioned Halloween to her some time ago but she had paid little attention to what he said. Now, with Halloween two weeks away, her curiosity is heightened.

As Melody and Roderick sit in the living room watching the 20-inch television set, a commercial is broadcast on Channel 9. It shows an animated large black bat flying toward the screen. It is apparently an advertisement for the upcoming movie, *Nightmare on Elm Street*. That commercial is followed by another: A girl is surrounded by white smoke in a cemetery, then a man suddenly appears on the scene dressed in black. This movie is *Dracula Returns*. The movie advertisements are followed by several commercials for Halloween candies and other paraphernalia.

"Roderick, what is Halloween, really? What is all this excitement," asks Melody, unable to contain her curiosity any longer.

"You ain't know what Halloween is, Mel? Don't you got Halloween in Jamaica?"

"And if we do, then why did I ask you?" Melody retorts, imitating her brother's American accent.

"So how come when I try to tell you one time before now, you act like you know and you didn't want to listen to me."

"No, we do not have Halloween in Jamaica, and it does not seem like fun to me anyway."

"Really, Mel! Well, it's lots of fun and scary too. The scary is the fun."

Roderick then explains all the myth and fiction he knows about Halloween -- about witches and goblins, and more. After he is finished, Melody emphatically informs him that she is not participating in any Halloween events and she is not wearing any costumes.

"But Mel, Halloween makes you be anything you want to be. A princess a . . . a anything you want, Mel."

"No! No princess, no witch, no nothing; after me no idiot or Jonkanoo," she replies with conviction and will not be convinced by her brother.

"What's Jonkanoo?" It is now Roderick's turn to be curious.

Melody takes a deep breath, gives a wide sly grin and begins to relate her account of all she knows about Jonkanoos back in Jamaica. "Jonkanoos come out at Christmas time and they are people who get dressed up in some funny-looking, real scary costumes. Just like Halloween costumes or even scarier . . . ." She pauses and gives her younger brother a sly look. "To be honest with you, Roddy, me never know that it is real people when I was real little. Nobody could convince me that Jonkanoo wasn't the real thing dem dress up like. For instance, the *horse head* and the *devil*, those were the two I was really afraid of."

"Anyway, as I was saying," she says, launching back into her 'Jonkanoo' description, "these Jonkanoos dress up into different-different costumes and beat drums and other homemade instruments and dance to the music. They don't stay in one place but move to different areas and people give them money. Sometimes they are miles away but you hear the drums from real real far, and you know the Jonkanoos, coming."

Melody rests her chin in the palm of her left hand and stares absent-mindedly with a grin on her face. She giggles hysterically for a few minutes, then calms herself down and tells Roderick about the time she ran from a horse head. She finds it difficult to compose herself while she relates this incident.

"It was Christmas Eve and Grannyma, Bubbles and me were in town shopping. I was about eight years old and Grannyma sent me over to the haberdashery store to buy some new cabinet doilies. A big horse head Jonkanoo came into the store and me never know seh me could run so fast, but one dash and I ran out the shop, straight home and went underneath the bed. Grannyma saw me running and told me to come to her, but all I said to myself was, 'foot, move faster'. When Grannyma came home, she was vexed with me because I didn't buy the doilies and she call me fool-fool"

Roderick laughs at his sister. "Sounds scary, but it still ain't sound like no fun to me. Halloween is better."

They sit and watch television a while longer, before going to bed, but every time Melody sees a commercial about Halloween, she shrugs her shoulder.

The week of Halloween brings more excitement and Melody is still not too enthusiastic about this new ritual she is about to experience in her new environment. On Sunday, the day seemed to go by quickly after Melody and Roderick returned from church. She watches some of her favorite sitcoms on television, then goes to bed after dinner.

On Monday morning, Melody wakes up the same time as usual, but she still feels sleepy. She looks over at the small clock radio on her nightstand. It reads 5:45 a.m. Bubbles is still sleeping and snoring noisily. "Bwoy! Something funny, it's only quarter to six. So how come me up so early."

She walks to the kitchen, where she bumps into her Dad who is fixing his lunch bag to leave for work. The kitchen clock reads 6:00 a.m., but it is deliberately set faster than the other clocks in the house.

"Melly" (Mr. Pennycook always called her by this name), what you doing up so early?"

"Me think it was time to get up, Dada. I always wake up at this time."

He smiles and looks at her. "A bet you Nel change the time for you last night when you sleeping."

Melody quickly clutches her pink robe with her left hand to keep it from opening, and puts her right hand over her face and opens her mouth disguising her frightened response.

"Ahoa! Me feget. Yes! We have to back the clock one hour since daylight saving time is done. No wonder me still feel so sleepy, for although my body is up, it is not 7:00 a.m. , as last week. Mi going back to sleep."

"Yes, me child, this is how we do it over here. We change the clock to suit the season. The custom is in October, you Fall backward, one hour behind, and in April, it is spring forward, one hour ahead. Is one thing me know seh doh, Almighty God is the only one that control and no man can control time. See you later, I have to leave now."

Melody says goodbye to her father and walks back to her room. She hopes to get another few minutes of sleep before 7:00 a.m. She removes her warm pink robe and lies down on her back on the bed, looking at her favorite poster of the Jamaican Coat of Arms. She closes her eyes tightly and counts sheep to fall asleep. She grins broadly, as she thinks, "America is really different in so many ways." On second thought, however, she realizes that that statement may need adjustment. "Well, Melody, America is the only other country you know, so don't be so broad in your statement," she admonishes herself. "Well, different from all the things I know in Jamaica. Yes sah! They . . . a mean we . . . since I live here now . . . can actually try to change the time! At least, so we think; but as Dada said, God's time don't change. Is only the clock setting change. Wait till me write Retti and tell her about this Halloween business and changing the time. Me can just imagine how she going to roll dem big bullfrog-looking eyes." Melody smiles again and drifts off to sleep.

"Mel! Mel! You not going to school this morning? You going to be late if you don't get up now."

Melody opens her eyes and sits upright on her bed, "Lawd have mercy! Thanks Bubs, me was up already, you know, and fell asleep again."

Bubbles is standing in front of her closet as usual trying to find an outfit to wear to school. "Ha! ha! Me did hear you when you get up, but me just ignore you 'cause me never want the sleep come out mi eyes," Bubbles responds with a silly giggle. "Sorry Mel, but I was up when Mama came in last night and changed the time for us, and the same thing she said she didn't want to happen, happened. She said all of us 'bout, 'bout yesterday and nobody remember to backset the clock."

* * * * * *

October 31st is finally here. It is Halloween! As Melody walks to school she is flabbergasted by what she sees. The windshield of cars and other vehicles are smeared with broken eggs. Rolls of toilet paper are strewn all over on trees and shrubs, littering the streets and sidewalks. People are dressed in different costumes, even those on their way to work, walking hurriedly to the subway stations. The Halloween tradition seems to be alive in every one around her.

"But anybody see me dying trial doh eeh!"

Melody did not say this out loud, but, as if reading her mind, Roderick says, "Told you Mel, Halloween is fun. Ain't this neat? Wow! Last night was goosie/mischief night."

"What night! This does not look right to me, no sah!"

Her brother explains mischief night, but Melody thinks it is still a ludicrous idea.

As they walk to school, Melody becomes more appalled every step of the way. However, she admits it is funny to see the weird and strange looking costumes the people are wearing. The schoolyard is exceptionally full of excitement. As she passes the Elementary School, she observes that the younger children are quite jovial. Melody tries hard to suppress her laughter. She stares, with a grin on her face, at some of the mothers who escorted their children to school. She sees a mother wearing a clown costume and can't help but be amused.

"But see yah, is what she favor? Dem no easy, atall," Melody thinks. "Mek me see, who dat one is?" she says, as she makes an attempt to identify another mother's costume.

The Junior High is no different from the Elementary, and as she walks to class, she chats with her two friends. "Are you going 'trick or treat'?" Ariel asks Melody, as they enter the room.

Roderick had explained that this was the fun part for most youngsters and some older children, too. They carried a Halloween bag (plastic), or any appropriate container to houses, stores or other business places, where they collected treats of candies and other edible items or toys. Roderick did not fail to explain that the tricks some people played at times turned out to be deadly.

"Yes, my father is taking my brother around the block. I think I will go with them to see what it is all about," Melody replies, glancing toward the front of the classroom, every now and then, in order not to miss attendance. "Are you going?"

Ariel and Kirk say no. Kirk, who sits the furthest from her, responds in a whisper, his lips rounded, expressing great emphasis. Ariel shakes her head while widening her big eyes to express the ridiculous feelings she has toward the idea.

Melody finds the atmosphere at school tantalizing today. Every so often, there are frightening yells coming from a girl or anyone, who been scared by another student wearing a Halloween mask. While at her locker getting some books for her next class, as Melody looks up from her combination lock, she comes face to face with an "alien" face-mask, similar in type to those she has seen on 'Star Trek' characters on television.

"Lawd, oh!" she says, loud enough for others to hear, and jumps back.

The kid wearing the mask quickly walks away, giggling. Those who witnessed the incident begin to laugh also. Melody does not consider the incident humorous, but wanting to hide her embarrassment gives a pseudo smile. On her way to class, she sees Kirk engaged in a conversation with a young brunette girl who seems to be held captive by his every word. A jealous wave sweeps over Melody. Her relationship with Kirk has been platonic, thus far, but deep within, she feels a slight passion for him.

"Hello, Melodie," Kirk calls out to her in his English accent, as he enters the classroom behind her, after saying goodbye to his friend.

"Hi!" Melody replies without looking at him and heads to her seat. Kirk immediately detects her aloofness. He is aware that something is wrong but has no time to explore the problem. Mr. Brandis asks the class to settle down quickly and get ready for the Math test they were told to prepare for. The class becomes really quiet as each student receives the test questions from the student in front of him or her. Some of the students, heads down, concentrate vigorously on the test questions. Others look up occasionally, while a few stare with a blank look at the board in front of them. Kirk glances at his friend Melody a couple of times, but her head is buried in her paper. He is anxious to find out what is bothering her.

The bell rings for the end of the period and some of the students give a sigh of relief. "O.K. class, bring all your papers to my desk. The homework assignment given yesterday will be reviewed tomorrow. Bet you all thought I didn't remember. WRONG!"

Melody moves towards Mr. Brandis' desk and Kirk follows behind, quickly.

"Come on, Melodie, are you ok?" Kirk asks, as he falls in step with her in the hallway.

"Yes. Why?"

"You know why, Mel! You are not your normal self, I'd say. Your response to me tells me something is wrong, my dear."

She stops and looks him in the eyes. The way he said 'my dear' flattered her and he sounded so mature for his age. "Well, since you ask and you are *so* concerned, who . . . who . . . ," she stutters as she frames the question. "Who was that white girl you were walking with?"

"Oh, so that's it! Oh! Oh!" He laughs as he speaks. "That is

Melissa from my drama club. Guess you didn't know I signed up."

"I see," Melody responds, skeptically. "Seems like Melissa is very glad to be in the drama club with an English chap."

Kirk understands now what may be going through her mind and is a bit flattered. He looks at her and gives her a singular smile, revealing his deep dimples and big white teeth. "Mel, dear, don't you worry your pretty little head. Remember, I am only fourteen years old and too young for that sort of thing. And I need to know more about American girls first. And if and when I need a date for whatever occasion, I think I will stick to my roots for now." He gives her a reassuring smile, as they separate to go to their next class.

Melody admits to herself that she feels much better than she felt when she saw Kirk with Melissa, forty-five minutes earlier. On the way to class, she approaches a group of five girls who are engaged in a loud conversation. They laugh heartily as they move around, demonstrating different poses.

"So, Miss W-a-n-d-a, you ready for this evening, girlfriend. What you gonna be for Halloween?"

"A girl of about 5ft. 5in. is walking around the others, hands spread away from the side of her body, as if she is modeling. Melody quickly glances through the crowd of girls and sees the girl she had encountered in the lunchroom. Now, she knows her name.

"Ama be Tina Turner. Got my boots and all. And I am ready. How about you, Lequisha?"

"Honey chile, I'm gonna be Winnie."

"Get outa here! You mean you goin' be Minnie like in Mickey and Minnie mouse. Girl, you are one sorry sista. Why you wanna be some cartoon kid stuff. Girl, get with it, Quish." Sherida, one of the girls in the group, is puzzled, thinking she heard the name Minnie.

Everyone bursts out in a boisterous laughter.

"Wait up, y'all. Excuse me, but Sister Lequisha ain't go'n be no silly cartoon character." She puts her hands on her hips and shifts her weight to the right. "I am goin' be Miss Winnie Mandela of South Africa, not Minnie! But y'all probably don't know who she is." She removes her hands from her hips and stretches them out in front of her letting them dangle as she continues to speak. "I know y'all is dumb and don't go to the Library and read books and that's why y'all think I was talking about some kid cartoon stuff."

"Yea! Lequisha, I know who you mean."

"Bet you do now, Nisie (Denise), cause I just done told you. See y'all later, Miss Tina, I mean Wanda Turner."

The four remaining girls quiet down as Lequisha walks away. They are about to resume their discussion but a teacher comes down the hallway and chases them off to class. Melody hears one of the girls swear silently at the teacher calling her an abominable name. She would not dare think of such words, much less say them. She shakes her head in disgust at the behavior of the young girls. "Bwoy dem out of order bad. Lord help me to continue to have respect for adults."

Melody notices Wanda, out of the corner of her eyes, looking at her, but she keeps on walking to her class.

At the end of the school day, Melody meets Roderick and they walk home together as usual. Roderick is impatient and hurries in front of his sister. He is anxious to put on his Halloween costume. This year, he will dress like He-Man the cartoon character with the big muscles – he is a hero who saves people. On their way home, they see children wearing Halloween costumes already on the street. Roderick's Dad promised to take him out after he gets home from work, eats dinner and relaxes a bit. Roderick has to do his homework first; and all this makes him more impatient.

As Roderick, Mr. Pennycook and Melody prepare to go on their mission, Roderick still begs his sister to wear a costume.

"No mi seh, me not looking like no *cunumunu*, me just walking with you and Dada."

"Look like what, Mel? I don't understand that word. Is that English?"

Roderick makes a face. His sister always throws a new Jamaican word at him.

"You don't worry what mi saying little brother, just understand that I am not dressing up in any costume tonight."

They step outside with Roderick leading the way in his He-man costume. They walk a few blocks, stopping at houses and stores where Roderick get treats. They run into other groups of costumed children, some carrying pillowcases or white plastic garbage bags to put their treats in.

Melody's attention is drawn to one person who is wearing a Dracula outfit and carrying a giant-size plastic bag. "But see here." She says to herself. "A weh him a go with that deh big bag. Him expect to gather all of Brooklyn tonight?"

They travel up and down most of the not-so-busy side streets, then they start towards home. Melody waits on the curb, while her Dad and Roderick make their last stop at a house they passed earlier on, because the lights were out. She sees a group of four Halloween masqueraders who are singing loudly as they walk in her direction. She recognizes the Tina Turner costume and knows it is Wanda. The other persons are dressed like Diana Ross and the Supremes.

"Hello, Miss Jemaikan!" Wanda steps up in front of Melody and sticks her Halloween bag in her face. "Trick or treat."

Melody tries to act friendly. "Sorry, but I don't have any treat, my brother has it all."

The girls give a scornful laugh and try to imitate her accent. "Listen to what she say, her *brodther* has it all. So where is your costume Miss Jemaikan. Is this it! What are you?"

Melody is not enjoying this now.

"I . . . I am just walking with my brother and father. I am not celebrating Halloween."

"How come!" They all chorused. "You live here, don't you?"

"Yes. But . . . ." She stops, realizing she doesn't have to explain to these girls.

"But what! You think you too cool or something?" Wanda is getting serious and picky. "Well, if you be so cool and different why you come to America then."

Melody is about to respond when Roderick runs down the steps to her excitedly. "Hey, Mel, I am loaded. Let's go. Can't wait to have a feast."

"Come on, Nissie, let's go. We ain't done yet." Wanda waves to her friend to move on.

Melody is not sure how to interpret Wanda's words. Is it a pun, meaning she (Wanda) is not done harassing her yet, or not done with trick or treat? She walks home in silence and goes directly to her room. In her room, she contemplates her several unpleasant encounters with Wanda and wonders if she should confront her. She is upset and bitter as she thinks.

"Should I continue to act normal and watch where . . . I don't even know what to call this situation . . . this is going? This Wanda girl, just

Mi Neva Know Sey

doesn't like me for whatever reason, and she sure shows it."

Melody realizes and accepts the fact that she is still fairly new in America. It has been only a few months and she still has a lot to learn about America. "Bwoy is a lot me never know 'bout since me come. But me never expect this little foolishness with this gal dem call Wanda. She smiles gingerly and, in an attempt to deal with her disappointment, makes a pun using Wanda's name: "A *Wanda* why she doesn't like me and I don't even know this pickney."

Melody pulls herself together and goes into the living room to watch television. She is determined to take her mind off the Halloween encounter with Wanda and her friends. Yet she cannot help but be concerned. This was the third time that Wanda's close presence has alarmed her and left a bitter taste in her mouth. An uneasy feeling. A curious "cannot understand" feeling. So far, since her arrival in America, most of her other school acquaintances have been pleasant and reasonably gregarious. Not many are buddy, buddy, but when she sees them, a friendly greeting is exchanged. Melody watches a re-run of the Lucy show, smiling occasionally when Lucy does something really funny. She then goes to her room and prepares for bed.

* * * * * *

Unlike Melody, Bubbles seems to assimilate into the American mainstream quite easily. She does not act like a new immigrant. Once, her Aunt Pansy even made the observation: "But Bubbles, if I didn't know you just come up, I would think you in America long time. You no easy, you fit in really well."

Bubbles is shorter than Melody. This has bothered her ever since they were kids. And it is no secret that Melody's long hair and her fair-skinned complexion have created some jealousy between them. But although she lacks these two distinct traits, Bubbles knows that she is just as attractive as her sister. The family's beauty is evident even in Grannyma who is in her sixties. Bubbles speculates that their mother got her good looks from their deceased grandfather Marks and Grannyma. She had seen their wedding photograph and could see her mother's resemblance to both of them. Both sisters realize that their mother's superb beauty had caused her to fall prey to the two men who had fathered them. Even a white man, (Melody's father) from a foreign country.

Bubbles' light brown hair of medium length is currently styled like her American friends. Her fashion is typically American and the clothes she wears make her stand out wherever she goes. Shortly after she started the ninth grade at Washington High, she had changed her style of dress to fit the American scene. She had saved up money from her lunch allowance and her small weekly allowance from her mother, to buy enough fashionable clothes to last her until the end of the year.

Bubbles is gregarious and has made many friends, both American and Jamaican who have been living in Brooklyn for a long time. Often, on weekends and sometimes in the evenings after school, she goes out with her friends. Mrs. Pennycook is concerned about her daughter's popularity and the friends she keeps and has spoken to her about these concerns.

"So, Bubbles, I see you fit right into America. Seems like you don't miss Jamaica atall," she commented, folding her arms in a protective gesture. "Take it easy though, me love. Mind the company you keep. Ah don't want you mix up, mix up with the wrong company, you know."

"Lawkes, Mama, man. You should know better than that. I could never let you and Granny down. Mi have me mind straight Mama. I know you going to compare me to Melody. But Mama, me and Melody is two different persons. Don't know who I take after," Bubbles had responded teasingly, and with a laugh, as she glanced at her mother.

Mrs. Pennycook is happy that Bubbles is doing well in school but her motherly instinct has caused her to be concerned about her social involvement. Whenever the phone rings, Roderick usually yells out, more often than not, "Bubbles! Your call." Even Roderick knows that she receives more phone calls than Melody.

One Saturday morning, Bubbles received a call, which Mrs. Pennycook answered. It was the same boy who had called many times before and she was curious. She approached her daughter, although she was a bit apprehensive in doing so, saying, "Seems like the fellow that keep calling like talking to you, Bubs."

"Who, Mama?"

"You know who me talking. The fellow who calls here very often. He sounds American, but sometimes you can detect a little Jamaican accent."

"Ahoa! That's Travis. He was born here, but his father is from Trinidad and his mother is from Jamaica. Yes, we are good, good friends, man."

"I see."

Her mother did not want to pry too much, so she did not asked too many questions.

* * * * * *

Bubbles returns home from the Halloween party, to which she had been invited, all geared up and excited. She had not worn an outrageous costume, but to be in with the crowd, she had dressed like a Jamaican flight stewardess. She had always admired them on the Air Jamaica commercial. She finds Melody in their bedroom, looking sad, like she had just seen a ghost.

"Melody!" she snaps. "Don't look so puney puney, you mek me feel that sometimes only me one get all the happiness. What happen now?"

"Nothing."

"Puleeaze!" Bubbles has caught on to this expression (please), like her friends say it.

"Me seh mi alright, man. Just tired."

Bubbles knows her sister well enough to know she is not telling the truth and prods her until she gives in.

"Since you insist. It is the same girl me tell you about at mi school. The one that don't like me feh nothing."

"What she do now?"

"She and her friends run into me when me follow Dada and Roderick trick or treat. And just her same mean feisty ways. And I don't know what me do this gal."

"Sis, mi hear what you saying, but you have to work this out for yourself. Mi know what me would do. And if she continue, mi we tell you what you must do." Bubbles looks at her sister and rolls her eyes expressing a stern look. "Just because me have all these friends, don't think seh mi don't study some of these school children too and see that some of them not nice."

Melody is shocked to hear Bubbles say that. She thought she was the only one having problems with some of the students. She is still trying to decipher why Wanda is so mean to her when she hasn't done her any harm. Back in Jamaica, all the things she heard about America were good and as a child she thought there were no flaws or bad things about this great country. Yes, she had heard of the struggles between Blacks and Whites and those social problems that exist like in any other country in the world. But she was younger then and did not understand too much or cared much about these things.

Now that she is in America, and being a black girl (albeit fair skinned), she is puzzled why Wanda acts like her enemy. The truth is, they are both Black and should be allies (so to speak), and not enemies. She is determined not to allow this little episode with Wanda stop her from going forward. She will make an effort to resolve this problem some way. She remembers her mother's instructions and admonitions and smiles now, as she remembers the words her mother pepped her up with. She does not say them out loudly, but in her heart she repeats them: "Duppy know who to frighten."

Bubbles is very tired and falls asleep during their conversation. She is unaware of the positive effect their conversation has had on Melody. Melody feels better and appreciates having a big sister to talk to. No matter how different their personalities are, she knows that nothing can come between sisters, especially when there is only one. Friendship and love between sisters are like bread and butter, she believes.

When Melody drifts off to sleep, she sleeps fitfully throughout the night and is frequently awakened by hallucinations of someone standing over her with a mask. She awakens in the morning, upset and convinced that it was her Halloween experience and her encounter with Wanda that affected her rest.

* * * * * *

With Halloween behind her, Melody now faces a whole new experience of life in her new environment. Election Day is the first Tuesday in November. Melody is aware of the importance of the day from the avalanche of political commercials on television and campaign posters displayed all over Brooklyn. This year brings the Presidential, Senatorial and Congressional elections to New York City. The young new immigrant, although only a teenager, notices that election time in America is quite different from what she experienced in Jamaica. She is impressed.

The advertisements are pretty straightforward and competitive. Each candidate, irrespective of the office he or she is running for, advertises his or her capabilities and promises. Melody is familiar with this aspect of election. She is quite cognizant of the political strategies used in the political arena. Each candidate brags that he or she is the best for the office. At her age, Melody cares very little about politics but, at the same time, when the time comes for her participation, she wants to be informed, so that she can make the right choices.

Melody notices that the difference between the elections in America and Jamaica lies in the overall election and voting procedure. Here, everything seems to run more smoothly and decently. Candidates condemn and reprimand each other, but there is no fighting or violence in the process. She likes that. In Jamaica and in other small Third World countries, elections can be quite a disaster.

School is closed for the day, and Melody is happy for another day off from school. However, she tries to hide her jubilation when Roderick confronts her. "Yea, Mel! Bet you are real happy to be home today eh!", he teases, as he walks pass her in the living room. " Real happy I bet, ' cause I know you ain't like school too much."

"Oh shut up, Roderick. What gives you that idea?"

"Come on, Mel. You know you not too crazy about school. I am just a kid, but you can't fool me."

Melody would never acknowledge what her brother says publicly, but she knows it is true that she does not like school. Not school in America, anyway.

Election Day passes smoothly and calmly. From the television evening news, Melody is made aware of the election process and voters choices. Voting booths showed no sign of problems or excitement. Voters stood in line and waited their turn to vote.

"This is one thing that I can say: Me never know sey Election Day can be so calm and peaceful. America, you impress me this time."

When Roderick walks into the living room, he sees his sister with her eyes glued to the television set and talking to herself. "There you go again, big sister, talking to yourself. How come you watching that boring stuff and you ain't even a grown up yet."

"Little brother, I am learning more and more about America every day. Why don't you leave me alone?"

The remaining school days for the week are routine and at the end of the school week, Melody is happy that there were no big problems or surprises. She did not encounter Wanda's picking on her. She now looks forward to going up to Connecticut for the weekend, with her family, to visit a cousin. Melody is adventurous and likes the idea of visiting another state.

Ah School!

November brings more cold weather to Brooklyn. Melody realizes there is no escaping the winter and each new day brings a new experience. She does not allow pride to direct her when she dresses for school. She ignores Roderick's ridicule and tells him that one day when he gets older, and his bones start to get old and feeble he will be sorry he didn't take care of himself when he was younger.

This will be a short week at school. Wednesday will be the last day, and although it is already Tuesday, Melody already finds the school week long and tedious. The month of November is designated as Teachers Professional Month, and school will be closed on Thursday and Friday to allow the teachers to attend educational seminars and workshops. Part of Melody's anxiety is due to her having difficulty with algebra. She was devastated by the C+ she received on the last test, for which she had barely studied. But Kirk is now helping her and she is confident that she will get over this hurdle.

Then there is the feeling of homesickness she has had for the last couple of weeks, which she cannot disguise. She misses her friends in Jamaica, and the country itself. Kirk told her that her feelings – the homesickness – is natural for this time of the year, and that it is called the winter blues. He has also explained that the colder it gets, the worse she will feel.

"It is too cold for me, sah! I don't know if I can survive this cold atall. I know it would be cold in America, but bwoy me never know sey it this cold."

"Come on, Melodie, it is not that cold. And it is not really winter yet." Kirk is used to the cold, having experienced it in England and Canada.

"How you mean is not winter yet, Kirk? So what you call this?"

"Oh, Melodie, you make it sound like you in the Arctic Ocean or Iceland. I hear that it gets really cold in late December through March. Yep! Zero temperature."

"But is what you a seh to me doh, eeh! You mean zero, like nought." She spreads her lips wide and lets them quiver as if she is freezing.

Kirk laughs. "Nought, I haven't heard that word in a long time.

Last person I heard said that, was my grandmother, when I went to see her in St. James, Jamaica. Yes, Melodie, nought, as in below the Farenheit scale."

Melody is not consoled, but rather becomes more depressed and homesick. She decides that she must be positive though and take one day at a time. When she finds herself making frequent trips to the bathroom during classes, she attributes it to the weather.

On one of these trips to the bathroom, while class is in session, she is surprised to find many students there. She wonders if the pending days off is having an affect on them also – "freedom fever," as she refers to it. Some students leave the bathroom as Melody enters, but the two stalls are still occupied. As she waits her turn, her bladder feels like it is ready to explode. She decides to use the bathroom on the first floor, although students are not allowed to leave the floor on which their assigned classes are held. "Mi will explain to the hall patrol that is either me die or do. But me can't wait anymore."

As she turns around to leave, a young girl walks out of the stall nearest to the window. She looks embarrassed and walks right past Melody and the sink without washing her hands. Melody gives a scornful look and goes into the stall. The odor is not pleasant. "Yes bwoy, this will knock me out, mek me hurry up and come out."

Shortly after the occupant of the other stall leaves, Melody hears two girls enter the bathroom talking in low tones. "Come on Wanda, hurry it up girl and let's get outta here before we get company. Gimme my Virginia Slims. I got the lighter." The new arrivals do not notice that one stall is still occupied.

"Quiet, Shevaune, you got to get used to this, then you won't be so nervous. First, we got to see if all the stalls are empty, 'cause we gotta go in them and do our smoke. See, you gotta flush the butt down the toilet when we done and open up the windows."

"Ok, so let's go. Gimme one."

Melody freezes. Her flow is cut. She peeps through the door crack and sees her adversary. She is a bit nervous and takes a deep breath. Her immediate reaction is to panic.

"Hey! Someone is in here, Wan. We in trouble. Why you told me ain't nobody here this time of the day, girl. What we go'in do now?"

"Shevaune, calm down. Probably it's some little coward. We can handle her. Do not worry your nervous black head."

Melody walks out gingerly and goes towards the sink to wash her hands. "Look who we got here. Miss white Jemaikan. Told you we can handle this. Well, hello, there, whatsyournameagain?" Wanda pretends she knows her name and forgot.

Melody, for the first time, decides to act bold and stand up to Wanda. "Excuse me, are you talking to me."

"Well, well, Miss Jemaikan is a wisey. Am I talking to you, Shevaune? No, I am talking to me. Of course, I am talking to you, ivory." She puffs on her Virginia Slims and blows the smoke in Melody's face, making her cough.

"Wanda. Yes, I know your name. I think I better get out of here. I have to get back to class." Melody dries her hands as she speaks, and moves towards the door.

"So you ain't telling me your name, ah! One thang I got to say to you before you leave. You tell nobody about what you ketch us doing. Or you be telling me your name, your mama's name and alla y'all name."

Melody is already out the door, walking faster than usual to get to her class. Now she is even more anxious to get out of school for the rest of the week.

On her way home from school, she thinks about the girls smoking in the bathroom -- and, of all persons, her *friend* Wanda! She is shocked and disappointed, although she is aware that smoking in America is a habit practiced by old and young. She had seen children as young as eight and ten smoking in public in Brooklyn. She had wondered if they were doing so without their parents' knowledge, but then, sometimes, she had seen them smoking right in front of their homes.

"Yes! What a person does at home or on the streets is his or her prerogative. But not in school, a place structured for discipline and learning. It nuh right atall."

She reminisces about Jamaica. She does not recall that students ever smoked on the school compound, much less inside the bathroom. "No Sah. The piece a beating dem would get would leave a mark for life."

She strikes up a conversation with herself as she nears home. "Now, me not saying all the school children was perfect. I would be lying, because there were some bad boys and girls who could fight and cause war. But when it come to certain school rules, well, they try to follow."

She remembers the time a boy from her class got a good beating with the bamboo cane because he had a knife on him at school. Dudley Tomlison could not convince Principal Samuels why he was carrying the knife, which had fallen out of the back pocket of his Khaki pants, onto the playground at recess time. The knife had fallen out of his pocket when he reached for his handkerchief. A teacher saw it and reported him to the Principal. Melody was near the Principal's office getting chalk for her teacher, when Dudley was being reprimanded by the Principal. She remembers the incident clearly:

"But, Mister Samuels, sah . . . " Dudley had attempted to explain having the knife. "Is because me forget it this morning in me pocket when me Grannie ask me to cut some calalloo, sah, just as me was leaving for school."

"Cut callaloo, when you have on your uniform already for school. Young boy, don't take me for a fool. I wouldn't be the headmaster if a never have any sense. Hold out you hand straight, boy. I have more important things to do."

Mr. Samuels was tall and looked stern. All the students were afraid of him. He gave four hot wallops with the cane to Dudley, until the palms of his hands turned red.

Melody is amused as she thinks about Dudley. Not about the punishment he received, because that was one thing she hated about school in Jamaica, but because Dudley had an accident when he was flogged. Poor Dudley had no choice but to return to class, although he was embarrassed. When he entered the class, all the students laughed when they saw his pants. Dudley told them he got sprayed by the hose when he was crossing the lawn, but they knew otherwise and nicknamed him "hose" after that day.

When she reaches home, Melody greets her mother absentmindedly, still engrossed in her thoughts, and goes directly to her room.

* * * * * *

Thursday morning finds Melody in bed, snuggled warmly under her blanket. She is very happy there is no school today or tomorrow. The temperature had dropped overnight and although her Dad turned up the heat during the night, she still feels chilly. She rolls over on her back and looks up at her window. It is smeared and condensed from the frost.

Mi Neva Know Sey

"Oooohweeeee!" She shivers deliberately. "Glad me not going to school today. It looks very cold outside." Her lips tremble mockingly as she speaks.

Melody rolls back onto her stomach and buries her face in her soft downy pillow with the intention of going back to sleep.

Bubbles who is also off from school is still sound asleep in her bed. Melody tries to ignore Bubbles' loud snores that seem to get louder by the minute.

Bubbles was recently diagnosed with deviated nasal septum and allergies. Their mother had detected that there was a problem, because Bubbles slept with her mouth open and often complained of earaches and headaches. No one was aware of her respiratory problems, although since she was a toddler, their mother (before she left Jamaica) and Grannyma had realized that there was something unusual about her breathing patterns. Melody remembers that at certain times of the year, when they lived in Jamaica, Bubbles would sneeze a lot, stick her right finger in her ear and twirl it around, while making a funny sound in her throat, like a cat's paw scratching at concrete.

Melody throws a pillow at her sister in an attempt to disrupt the snoring, but Bubbles only closes her mouth for a second, then resumes snoring. Since school is closed today, Melody tries to fall asleep again, because it is too early to get up. She hears her father leaving for work and feels sorry that he has to face the cold. "Better him than me, though," she thinks. "Him use to it, him here long time." She eventually falls asleep again while staring at her Jamaican Coat of Arms poster.

Melody jumps at the sound of her name, as she awakens with a lingering smile on her face.

Her mother, who has just entered the room, is curious. "Is what sweet you so, Mel? You have a phone call. I think it is yuh friend Kirk."

"Cho Mama, man, you just wake me out of a nice nice dream. Guess where mi was? Right back on Peanut Lane in sunny, sunny Spanish Town. Me and Retinella was going to the shop and I stopped and was talking to mi other friend Peggy, and Retinella called out to me, to come on. That's when you called mi name."

She yawns, as she goes to answer the phone.

"Hey, Melodie! What are you up to? Got any plans for the days off?" Kirk asks.

"Kirk it is early, I am still relaxing, taking it easy. Man! You don't know how good it feels to be off from school for a day . . . much more two days. Mi learning at school . . ." she pauses, "but Kirk, school in America is a rough place."

"There you go, Mel, my reason for calling. Want to go shopping with me and my cousin Clemente. He been here a long time and he knows a lot of places."

"Kirk, you crazy! Me and two men go shopping! No sah."

"I am ahead of you, Mel. Knew you would be skeptical. My cousin Daliha, Clemente's sister, will come too. She is sixteen."

"A'right. When you coming to get me? I have to get ready."

"About 12:30, 1:00 p.m. Be ready, Mel! See yah."

Melody goes back to her room and begins writing two letters, one to her cousin Eunice and the other to her friend Retinella. The letter to Eunice is short and to the point, but she realizes that she is going to need more time to write and update her best friend. She starts the letter to Retinella: *Dear Retti, how are you doing today? I hope when these few (well not few) lines reach you, it will find you ok. Well me dear, guess what? Today and tomorrow I do not have to go to school . . . my crazy school, because we get the days off. Retti, I am trying to make it, but it is very different in school here . . . .* She stops and glances at the clock, and sees that time is going by quickly. She will finish her letter on Friday.

She gets dressed, then goes into the living room where Roderick is seated watching his favorite shows. He glances at her and laughs. "Galee! Mel, you ain't going to the North Pole, you know. Come on, it ain't that cold out there."

She knows she looks like a mummy, all wrapped up from head to foot in her winter gear. She is wearing a blue wool hat with earmuffs to protect her ears, with a matching blue scarf and gloves. Under her brown knee length boots she is wearing leg warmers and socks.

"So you think. Me not taking any chances."

The doorbell rings at 12:45 p.m. It is Kirk. "Bye Mama. Bye Roderick. See you all later."

Kirk looks at her and bursts out laughing. "Jolly! Mel, don't believe any cold breeze can get to your body."

"Shhh! Be quiet. Not you too. We going shopping in the cold, right?"

Mi Neva Know Sey

They sit in the back seat of the Toyota Corolla while Daliha sits in front with her brother. Kirk introduces Melody to his cousins, who are also amused by her outfit.

The first stop is, the King's Plaza Mall near the Flatbush Section of Brooklyn, which is well known for its bargains. However, Clemente's main stop is the Green Acres Mall on Long Island.

"The place big you see. Whole heap of stores, and everything under one cover. Mi like that better, man." Clemente has a heavy Jamaica accent although he has been living in America for a while.

"Me like that too, man. At least, it will keep me out of the cold," Melody responds, in a down to earth way to accommodate Clemente's heavy Jamaican dialect.

Kirk nudges her with his elbow and smiles. He is happy she feels comfortable with his family.

When they arrive at the Green Acres Mall, the parking lot is crowded, even though it is Thursday, a weekday, but they manage to find a spot close to the entrance.

"How come this place so crowded and it is not Saturday. This country is something else! People never tired to shop and keep busy all over the place it seems," Melody exclaims, repeating her favorite line, silently,

"Bwoy, me never know sey!"

There is a mass of people in Alexander's Department store. Melody and her friends soon realize that there is a big sale there -- this is the reason for the crowded parking lot.

Clemente takes the initiative to make some rules and gives the "children" some instructions. "Ah right, this is what we going to do. We split up and meet right back here in three hours." He looks at his watch. It is now 2:30 p.m. "Be back by 5:30 p.m. Kirkie, you and Melody stay together and Miss Daliha, you are on you own. But, remember, be back on time!"

Melody has some money on her, but she does not intend to shop a lot, only if she finds something that grabs her attention. She is only there because Kirk invited her. Unlike her sister, she is not a spendthrift. She has been saving up her allowance for a rainy day.

Kirk has some money, too. He wants to find a birthday gift for his Mom, whose birthday is not too far away, on December 16th. "Got to find a little something for me Mum, since I am here. Don't know if I will get the chance again soon to go shopping," he says.

Kirk and Melody walk around the mall, from store to store, window shopping and in search of a gift for Kirk's mother.

"Why don't you get your mother a nice scarf or gloves. She'll like that, and even if she has some already, hey, she'll have more to choose from," suggests Melody.

"Gee, thanks, Mel. It is always good to have a woman around."

Melody is flattered and responds with a what-can-I-say shrug.

Kirk picks out a pair of delicate black wool gloves for his mother and, as they stand in line for the cashier, Kirk's stomach makes a loud rumble. He puts his hands on his stomach and says loudly for Melody to hear.

"I wish this line moves faster. I think I am hungry."

They both agree that they are hungry, so after paying for the gloves, they walk back towards Alexander's and stop at the Woolworth's store nearby. Kirk remembers snacking at the luncheon counter on an earlier trip to Green Acres Mall with his mother. He knows the food there is affordable and delicious. They sit at the high stools at the counter, which faces out to the other departments of the store, and order pieces of southern fried chicken, some soft bread rolls and fruit punch.

"Umm! This is delicious," Kirk says, biting into his chicken leg and licking his finger.

"Yep! Not bad at all," Melody responds, distractedly.

Her attention is drawn to the watch repair counter not far from the luncheon area. There, a middle-aged, medium height woman is talking loudly to the mail clerk who is behind the counter. The clerk, who is Caucasian, is somewhat older than she is, white-haired, tall, slim and wearing suspenders. Both face Melody and Kirk, so their voices project easily in their direction. The conversation gets heated and the woman's voice gets louder. Melody recognizes the woman's Jamaican accent.

"But when a call, dem tell me seh the watch ready and I should come pick it up today. Now you telling me it not ready, sah. A leave me house early, you know sah, and stop here before a go to me job. Only feh hear the watch not ready!"

"I am sorry, Miss . . . ."

She cuts him off. "Yuh sorry, how you mean yuh sorry?"

The old man still has his mouth open in anticipation of getting a word in. "As I said, I apologize for the error. Your watch will be ready on

Saturday, Miss. I am extremely sorry."

"Sattiday, clear 'til Sattiday. But if anybody see me dying trial, eeh. I can't understand unoo people."

She is really making a scene and shoppers linger to watch and listen. The lady argues, directing some heavy Jamaican words at the clerk, who does not understand most of what she is saying. Melody smiles to herself and turns to Kirk, who is also as baffled as the old man.

"Now that is how some Jamaicans are, they like to vent and get it all out. She knows the American man doesn't understand all of what she says but it makes her feel lighter to tell it like it is."

Melody smiles and thinks of all the things she has experienced in America so far. This experience with the Jamaican lady and her conflict with the American clerk is only another to add to her growing list of "me never know sey". Never in her wildest dreams could she imagine seeing this kind of behavior in America.

"You tek dem out of the country, but you can't take the country out of dem," she muses. She remembers the old saying and sees how applicable it is to what she has just witnessed. She personally believes the woman should have been a little easier on the poor old man.

Kirk looks at his watch. "Oops, we better go. It is time to meet Clemente and Daliha."

They hurry to the designated spot where Clemente told them to meet. Three minutes later, Clemente joins them, but they have to wait another ten minutes for Daliha. When she arrives, her brother growls at her and promises never to take her with him again. As Clemente turns his head away, Daliha cuts her eyes and sticks out her tongue at him.

Leaving the mall is a hassle. It seems like, by arrangement, all the shoppers have decided to leave at the same time. What should have been a two-minute exit from the mall, turns into fifteen minutes. Eventually, they access the Brooklyn-Queens Expressway and are on their way home. It was a long day for Melody, but she enjoyed it all. In any case, it was surely better than being in school.

* * * * * *

On Friday morning, Melody sleeps late. She is determined not to leave the house today. She gets up around 11:00 a.m., eats a late breakfast, then goes back to her room to finish her letter to Retinella. She writes six pages, giving her friend an update on everything, including her trip to the mall.

When the four days off (Thursday and Friday, plus the weekend) from school end on Sunday night, Melody admits she truly enjoyed every minute of it.

* * * * * *

Monday morning finds Melody in a state of lethargy. She believes it is caused from being off from school for so many days. She decides not to go school too early, to avoid standing in the line in the cold waiting to go inside. Her aim is to get there just before the bell rings, for the students to go inside.

As she walks to school, she grumbles to herself: "This is craziness man, how could the school authorities stick to a stupid rule like this. Dem want you feh stand up inna the cold and catch pneumonia! Mi really think seh in the winter time dem would make exception to this outside waiting business." She is really infuriated at the idea that even in the cold, the students still have to wait outside until the bell rings.

She reflects on her sunny homeland, walking in the balmy weather. It was better in Jamaica, except when it rained. There was no need to worry about the weather changing because of the seasons. She misses the tropical climate; she had been familiar with. But, ironically, she looks forward to the adventure of passing through the four seasons; this, too, would be part of her new experience in America.

"Mi know seh it nice to experience the seasons in action in America. Yes, it kinda nice. I used to read about it in storybooks and see it on television back home. And, yes, now I am a part of it," Melody tries to console herself, and shivers as a cold breeze brushes her face. "But bwoy mi really never know sey dem would let me poor pickney gal stand out in the cold like this and freeze."

She is startled out of her thoughts as Ariel touches her shoulder.

"Hey, Melody! You looka lost. You OK?"

"Yes, man. Just cold, Ariel. This cold makes me think of home, man."

"Si. Comprende, Melody. America is cold. Yes cold. Muy cold in the winter time."

Melody smiles at her friend speaking both in Spanish, and English at the same time

* * * * * *

Mrs. Varma is not in the classroom and the students are really noisy, and unruly. It is almost time to salute the flag and, still, Mrs. Varma has not arrived. Melody is concerned. She is about to share her concern with her two friends, when a young, dark-haired white woman walks into the room, out of breath.

"Sorry, I am late. The principal switched the room on me at the last minute."

"Yes! A substitute," Jerron Thomas yells out, loud enough for Melody to hear. "Got me a free period today."

"Oh, no, not a substitute. The class going to be bad, today." Brooke Paige is worried. She is sitting in front of Melody.

Melody is not sure what is going on, but concludes from all the excitement that the young woman, who looks around twenty-five years old, is taking over the class. She also infers that most of her classmates are happy about this turn of events.

"O.K., it is time for the pledge; let us all stand now." The substitute teacher tries to calm the class down.

The class stands up noisily and half the class does not repeat the pledge. Jerron and his friend Felipe are engaged in a quiet conversation and others are disengaged. Only a few of the students are paying attention. As Melody observes all this, it does not take her long to figure out that the substitute teacher is not respected. She wonders why.

Roll call is a disaster. Melody cannot believe her eyes and ears. Except for a few of the students, no one seems to answer to his or her name. Some barely raise their hands high enough for the "sub" to see. Others just ignore her and the "sub" only identifies whom they are by someone else pointing them out. After she is finished with roll call, she writes her name on the chalkboard -- Miss Knickerbocker. The response is a sardonic laugh from the majority of the class.

Miss Knickerbocker is not enjoying this, but is determined to be a teacher. After all, this was the reason she majored in English. She had done her student teaching while in her junior year at Syracuse University, in upstate New York. It had been a challenging experience, but she was determined to make teaching her career.

Mrs. Varma's class (for which she is substituting) first period, is English. The Substitute teacher was told that the class is currently studying American literature. However, needless to say, Miss Knickerbocker is having some difficulty controlling the class.

"I believe we are studying Hawthorne, aren't we?" asks Miss Knickerbocker, in an attempt to peak the student's interest.

There is a guttural sound from half the class as they open their books. "Hey, Miss Knicks. Why we got to study about no dead man and all that stuff he write a long time ago?" This is from Jerron Thomas, who is well-known for his critiques.

"Well, I believe Mrs. Varma already explained all this, and about the importance of literature, when she started the curriculum. So just let us move on. You will learn to appreciate it some day."

She senses the challenge and the opposition. The Substitute is cautious not to be trapped by it. "Hawthorne's, -- <u>The House of the Seven Gables</u> that is what you are reading now. Correct. Can someone give me a summary of the story so far."

Brooke Paige's hand is up. She is a quiet Black American girl who is smart. Melody admires her behavior and sometimes joins her at lunch. When she first heard the name "Brooke", Melody had repeated it silently. "Brook! Is what kinda name that? Somebody can name Brook? Bwoy dem have some funny names over here sah."

As far as Melody knew, a brook was a stream, and, as a proper name for a girl, it sounded strange to her the first time she heard it. She had asked another classmate to spell her name. When she saw that it was spelled differently from the familiar stream reference, Melody realized then, that it was beautiful name. She loved the name since that day, and even pondered that she would use it one day.

Brooke sits forward in her chair as all heads turn toward her. She gives a summary of Nathaniel Hawthorne's story, citing the main characters, in her deep Brooklyn accent, struggling to sound formal.

"Bravo, Bravo, Brooke. Go Brooke." Isaiah Thomas cheers. "That's my home girl, y'all."

After a short discussion, with contribution from other interested students, the bell rings and the period ends. The fall out is worse than when Miss Varma is in charge. Miss Knickerbocker places her hand on her forehead expressing a sigh of relief and Melody walks up to her with sympathy. "Are you coming back tomorrow, Miss?"

"I don't know. It all depends if your teacher will be back. Why?"

"Well," Melody pauses. She does not know how to express her sympathy and not sound rude. "This is really my first time . . . you see, I am new from Jamaica and it is the first time I have a class with a substitute. And I don't like how the other students behaved. Really, Miss."

"What is your name, again?" Miss Knickerbocker detected that Melody is from Jamaica even before she tells her.

"Melody Pennycook, Miss."

"Melody, thanks for your concern, but don't worry, dear. I am used to this. Did it before, while I was in university."

Melody blushes. She wonders if the teacher thinks she is weird.

"O.K, Miss, I have to run to my next class now. Bye."

"Bye, Melody. See you again. Maybe."

On her way to class, Melody holds her books closely to her chest, and is deep in thought. "Lord have mercy on poor me St. Catherine thirteen-year-old girl. Is what this me live feh come see! What an awful set of children. Today dem turn wild. Behave like leggo beast; well, not all, but some."

Melody sees Kirk coming from his locker and they walk to their next class together. Kirk too is shocked at the students' behavior and agrees with Melody that they were very disrespectful.

"Don't ever recall that students behaved so rudely back in England. Mind you. We do have some very unruly ones, but I don't ever remember them behaving like this." Kirk's British accent is firm and he is very serious.

"Same way back in Jamaica, Kirk. The children have to behave in class, else them get caning. And after getting a beating with cane once, nobody in their right mind wants to feel it again." She pouts in disgust as she recalls the first time she got a cane beating. "Yes, is one time I ever get caning and it was not deserved."

She recounts to Kirk the story of the caning she received in school back in Jamaica. She had arrived late at school because her grandmother was very sick. She and Bubbles had to care for Grannyma, until their grandaunt, Icilda arrived from Chapelton. Kirk listens thoughtfully and agrees that the caning was unwarranted.

This initial experience with a substitute leaves a bitter taste in

Melody's mouth and she hopes she doesn't have this experience again. But she is aware that this is inevitable, since a teacher may be absent for various reasons. "Only hope the next time it is a man. Maybe him can handle them better," she resolves.

The morning already feels like a whole day for Melody, but she is happy that today is only half a day. School is being dismissed early for Parent/Teacher conferences. It is the end of the First Marking Period. The conference will be held in two sessions; one from 1:00 p.m. to 3:00 p.m. and the other from 6:15 p.m. to 8:15 p.m. Report cards were already sent home and the conference is open to all parents who want to speak to the teachers about their children's progress. The school board has arranged the hours to try to accommodate all parents.

Although Melody and Roderick are doing very well in school, Mrs. Pennycook plans to attend the conference because she wants to show the school officials that she is a concerned parent and an educational advocate for children. Above all, she wants to have a one-on-one dialogue with Melody's teacher to find out how her daughter is adjusting to her new school. In order to attend the conference, she has switched her day off with a co-worker.

"Are you coming with your parents to conference tonight, Melody?" Kirk asks as they leave class.

"Umm . . . I don't know, yet. I think so. Mama wants me to come with her."

"I will definitely be here. So I guess I'll bump into you. See you, later, Melody."

* * * * * *

When Melody arrives home, she smells a nice aroma coming from the kitchen. "Good afternoon, Mama. Is it what I think it is, you are cooking?"

She goes over to the stove and opens the big Dutch pot. "Uh huh! Yes, bwoy, stew peas!"

Red kidney beans cooked with salted pig's tail and salted beef (known to Jamaicans as stew peas) served with white rice is a household Jamaican favorite; at least for those who set aside health concerns and skepticism about eating certain kinds of meat. In the Pennycook household, everyone loves stew peas, especially Roderick, who terms himself a *Ja-merican*.

"Ja-merican!" Melody repeated the term with curiosity the first time she heard her brother used it while talking to his friend Dante Dixon on the phone.

"Yea, Mel," Roderick had replied with emphasis. "I am a Ja-merican. Half Jamaican and half American."

"Please, stupid. You cannot be half Jamaican and half American. You were born here, so you are an American citizen. However, it is better to say you are an American born to Jamaican parents. Or, an American with a Jamaican culture or background. Not any half this and that," Melody had explained, attempting to correct him.

Roderick had tried to defend his theory that day, but resolved that his sister was right, since she is older.

Melody goes to her room where she sits on her bed and daydreams for a while. She can see and hear, vividly, what she experienced earlier in her class with the substitute teacher. "A dead donkey would get up and kick me if I tell him how the children behaved today. Mi never know sey little pickney can act that way." She smiles to herself, amused at the memory of the old Jamaican cliche.

She flops back with a thud on her bed, stretching out on her back. A sudden drowsiness comes upon her and she falls asleep. When her mother awakens her, it is not clear to her how long she had slept, but she knows for sure the nap was refreshing.

"So Melody, me love, what if you were still at school? Is so you would be sleeping in class?" Mrs. Pennycook asks, as she awakens her.

Melody yawns lazily and stretches her hands over her head trying to shake off the inertia. "No, Mama. No way! You can't sleep in school. Plus me would be embarrassed."

She yawns again and remembers that one student, her classmate Debbie Smith, always sleeps in class. "I don't know why mi feel so tired. And you still want me to come with you tonight, right?"

"Of course. That is why mi come tell you to come eat some dinner so that we can leave soon. Mi want to be one of the first parents there. 'Cause I know seh plenty parents going to show up tonight."

Melody walks to the bathroom and rinses out her mouth, then goes into the kitchen to enjoy her stewed peas and rice dinner. She really does not want to go outside again because it is very cold and, usually, once she is home from school, she likes to stay indoors. She is consoled however, that her Dad is driving them to the school, although it is only a few blocks down the road.

When they arrive, the auditorium is almost packed with parents, teachers and some students. Melody surveys the crowd. She sees a mixed group -- a cross-section of Blacks, including West Indians, Whites, Hispanics, and Jews. America is truly the Melting Pot she heard about.
She recognizes the West Indians because they seem to carry a marked profile about them, and by their dialect. She also recognizes the Jews because of the way that some of them dress. There is a Jewish boy in her class and, when she first saw him, she had inquired about the little black cap he was wearing. It is worn by the observant, or Orthodox Jews and it is known as a 'Yarmulke'.

Melody and her mother try to find a seat close to the stage where the Principal, Mr. Powers, will give his opening remarks, but also close to the exit.

Mr. Powers tapped the mike to test the PA system. It echoes throughout the room. "Good evening, ladies and gentlemen, boys and girls. Welcome to our first student conference, for this school year."

There is hush in the room. "Thank you all for coming. Together, we will work to prepare our children for tomorrow. Your presence here tonight makes a difference."

The principal explains the agenda for the conference. After the assembly, Melody and her Mom quickly move towards her homeroom on the second floor to see Mrs. Varma, who is also her English teacher. Melody wonders if Mrs. Varma will be there, considering she was absent from class earlier.

"Lawkes, man. Two parents here already! Me think me would be the first one."

Mrs. Pennycook is a little disappointed. Two parents are ahead of her, and she suspects they did not go to the auditorium first. She notices that they both have a baby in the stroller beside them. "Mek dem go on. Poor thing. Them probably couldn't get a babysitter, so them hurrying." She sympathizes.

"She is here. Wow!" says Melody, when she sees Mrs. Varma at her desk.

"Who?" Her mother is curious.

Melody is happy that Mrs. Varma is okay and tells her mother about the substitute. She learns later from her teacher that she was absent because she had a very important errand to run. Mrs. Varma explained that she would not miss the students' conference, because it meant a lot to her also. Mrs. Varma is conversing intensely with one of the ladies with the stroller who appears to be in her late twenties or early thirties.

"Yes, Ms. Smith, I am a bit concerned about your daughter Debbie myself. She does not look her normal self. Is everything alright at home?"

"Miss Holmes, teacher. Not Smith, I am not married to Debbie's father." Melody is now aware that the lady is the mother of her classmate, Debbie Smith.

"I am sorry, Ms. Holmes. I just assumed."

"No, it's alright. Haven't seen him since she was five years old. I was only eighteen when Debbie was born."

Mrs. Varma is blushing. She is aware that everyone is overhearing this conversation. She has always disliked the lack of privacy at these conferences. On the other hand, she also realizes that it is not a counseling session and parents should not choose the conference to discuss private matters. Melody's ears stand at attention as she listens to every word of the conversation between her teacher and her classmate's mother. She, too, has been noticing Debbie, who is always nodding in class and looks droopy all the time.

"Yes, Mrs. Varma. I knows I ain't too smart and all. Dropped outta school at seventeen. Never graduated High School, but I don't want my daughter to be like me."

She looks again at the report card in her hand. "Can't fool myself, teacher. Debbie ain't doing right. And she wasn't failing this bad last year. I know she ain't have it all up there but she ain't never get all D's."

"I understand your concerns, Ms. Holmes. I will try to talk to her and help her the best way I can. I will do my best."

"I sure appreciates it, Mam. I don't want my daughter to end up struggling like I am doing and that's why I am here. I know my time is up . . . appreciates your time. Thank you, Mrs. Varma."

Debbie's mother turns aside and Melody sees the sadness and the look of concern on the young mother's face as she fastens her young child in the stroller and leaves the room. The conference with the next parent is brief and then it is Mrs. Pennycook's turn.

"Good evening, Mrs. Varma," Mrs. Pennycook greets the teacher delightedly.

"How are you?" Mrs. Varma does not address her by a last name. She is cautious this time, not wanting to make the same mistake she made with Debbie's mother.

"Mrs. Pennycook. Yes, I am Melody's mother, teacher."

"Good evening, Mrs. Pennycook, pleased to meet you. And hello, Melody."

Mrs. Varma is quite elated in her greeting to Melody. She takes out her students' record book and a copy of the report card and scans them while looking over her glasses. "And . . . you are here because . . . ," she smiles, "you are proud of Melody or because you want Melody to do better." She smiles again.

"You are right, teacher, I am proud. And I cannot push her any harder. I think she is doing great, ma'am. But it is her first time in the school and you probably know that she is only in this country since June. And I just want to let you know and show you that I support her . . . all my children, a lot in their education." She smiles coyly and continues, "To be honest with you teacher, I was a bit worried and nervous when she started school. Didn't know how she was going to handle it atall because it is so different here than in Jamaica."

Mrs. Varma listens attentively to Mrs. Pennycook and is amused by her accent and expressions. She concedes the fact that she likes to hear Jamaicans speak, particularly the women. Her husband Jake works with a Jamaican man, who is also a good friend and when he comes over to hang out with her husband, she is never tired of listening to his sing-song accent.

"Well, like I said, and as you can see, your daughter is doing fine in all her classes. She didn't have a problem adjusting to the academics in America." She lowers her head, again, looking over her glasses at Melody. "Melody is a very bright girl and if she continues, she will make it. She did have a little problem the first couple of weeks but she got over that hump immediately."

"She did!" says Mrs. Pennycook, surprised.

"Oh, Mrs. Pennycook, do not be alarmed. It was a simple problem, which wasn't her fault. It was just the way she was taught in Jamaica, that's all. You see America is different in many ways and the spelling and pronunciation of certain words are some of the differences."

Mrs. Varma explained how she corrected words like: *colour* to color, *honour* to honor and assisted in the pronunciation of schedule, as in (sckedule) so Melody could adapt her vocabulary to the American style. "By the way, since you are here, I need to mention something to you which is going to be a surprise to Melody." She pulls both of her lips in together and licks them in an alluring manner.

"There is a competition coming up in December. An Essay Competition, and I would like to have Melody represent our school."

Melody's eyes pop open widely, as if she has seen a ghost.

"Told you it would surprise Melody." Mrs. Varma continues, "I will need your approval, Mrs. Pennycook, because it is going to be out of town, in Washington, D.C., and it requires an overnight stay, on Friday and Saturday nights. Your daughter really impressed me the first time she wrote an essay and many times after that. I like her style. When she wrote the essay on the first day of school (How I spent My Summer), she really expressed herself well."

Melody's big eyes again widen. She was unaware that the essay had really impressed her teacher that much. As a matter of fact, she now recalls wondering if Mrs. Varma would think she was being too bold.

"As I said before, you should be very proud to have a daughter like Melody. Continue to support her, and your other children as well. I am glad I am able to meet you and mention this to you. I know Melody is still trying to adjust to the American way and is still a bit shy and afraid. So please try to support her in this endeavor, which I am sure will be a great experience."

"I don't know what to say . . . I mean, sure she can represent the school. Well, thanks for thinking so highly of my daughter." Mrs. Pennycook is happy and a little beside herself. "Thank you for your time, teacher, and I do have another older girl in high school and a younger son, who is in the second grade. I am going to see his teacher now at his school."

Mrs. Pennycook and Melody walk quickly around the block to the Elementary School. The Brooklyn mother is happy that both schools set the same schedule.

The conference with Roderick's teacher is short. He, too, is doing well in school, but his behavior needs a little cleaning up.

"I believe you, Ms. Washington, Roderick talks a lot at home also. I will talk to him when I get home," Mrs. Pennycook assures Roderick's teacher.

When Melody and her mother go outside, Mr. Pennycook is nowhere in sight. "Is where Winston is doh, eeh? Mi tell him what time we would be ready and him not here. The very same thing that mi expect would happen, happen."

"Him soon come, Mama. You know how Dada stay a'ready. Don't like to sit around and wait. A bet him leaving the house five minutes later to make sure we ready when him come."

They are about to seek shelter from the cold in the building when the tooting of a horn stops them. It is Mr. Pennycook.

"Winston, you forget what time mi tell you fe come, noh? Mi tired you know, ah working all day around the house and then come straight to school. Cho, man."

Winston does not respond to his wife's complaining. He knows better than to try to defend himself. Melody smiles surreptitiously because she knows her Dad fell asleep and that is why he arrived late. He also knows he is guilty and is keeping a low profile. Mrs. Pennycook updates her husband on the teachers' comments about Melody and Roderick while they drive home. He can't help but beam with pride at their progress.

"A'right, Melly, don't stop working hard now, you nuh. When you leave high school, ah want you to get scholarship to the best university." He gives a quick glance over his shoulder and smiles at his daughter.

* * * * * *

Roderick goes into his sister's room as soon as they return home. "Hey Mel! Did you like conference night? I hate it. What did my teacher tell Mama about me, ah Mel?" he asks, without pausing for a breath.

"Slow down, baby brother. Take a breath. What do you have to worry about? You are a very, *very* good behaving boy. The best in the class, right?" Melody teases him.

"Yea! Right. I know what Ms. Washington told Mama." He looks worried and pitiful. "She always be saying I talk too much, but it is not true. It's Dante. He be the one that's always be talking to me. Then when I answer, she catches me."

"I am not your mother, Roderick. Don't be explaining to me. I am your sister, remember."

"I bet your teacher had a lot of good things to say about you. But your day will come, Mel, when you get a mean old teacher."

Roderick paces the floor as he plays his He-Man game. "Shute! I get good grades. I am smart. Hey, smarter than most of the kids in my class. A few of my friends, they be getting real bad grades and they hide the report card from their parents."

Melody turns to face him, surprised at what he just said. "Did you say hide report cards? Like not showing their parents? You kidding me!"

"Nope! I ain't. They like, kinda lie, you know, that they lost it or something and sometimes they get away with it. And their parents don't even bother to check with the school."

Melody finds it hard to believe, but she admits anything is possible with the children in America. She knows that neither she, nor her siblings, could pull this kind of stunt on their parents.

* * * * * *

The next day at school, Melody greets her friends Kirk and Ariel.

"Hey, Kirkie! How come I didn't see you at the conference last night?"

"Blimey, Melodie. I didn't make it after all. Me parents had an emergency at the last minute. How was it?"

"It was fine. My mother saw Mrs. Varma and they talked."

Melody is reluctant to tell her friends about the essay competition, for which her teacher had recommended her. Although she has bonded in friendship with Ariel and Kirk, she is still cautious about discussing certain matters. A reservation, which goes back to her childhood upbringing: Grannyma had instilled certain precautions in Bubbles and Melody. Kirk and Ariel will find out at the right time, she opines. And the revelation, she believes, should come from Mrs. Varma or someone else, because she knows that jealousy has no respect for friendship.

PART TWO

School Shock

The November temperature varies between 30 degrees and 35 degrees, but the sun never ceases to shine. When indoors, it is not difficult for one to be deceived by the brightness of the sun and expect warmth when one ventures outdoors. Melody has been a victim of such an illusion. One Saturday morning, at about 11:00 a.m., she woke up to brilliant sunshine. As she got out of bed, she stretched her hands above her head in an attempt to shake the feeling of malaise she had been experiencing recently.

"What a way the sun bright this morning, eeh! Must be nice and warm outside. Mi probably can go by the Library today since it is not that cold."

She had changed out of her nightgown, washed her face and, deciding to check the mailbox for letters from Jamaica, stepped out onto the small porch, without a jacket. A passing cold breeze hit her freshly washed face and passed through her entire body, forcing her to run quickly back inside. She was perplexed.

"But see ya doh, eeh! But it cold bad. America no easy. Look how bright the sun is, but it still cold like ice."

As a result of that experience, Melody learned not to be fooled by the sun during the winter. But despite the cold, dreariness of the season, she made a decision to accept the fact that the changing of the seasons is a gift from Mother Nature. "God is really great, bad! Look how Him just control everything when He wants to. At least that is how I see it. God controls the world, who want to believe it or not."

Most of the foliage is gone from the few trees in the neighborhood. The environment looks dead and barren. Only the evergreen trees and shrubs that border the front lawns of homes remain green. And certain places like New Jersey, the Garden State, have lingering colorful leaves on the trees. One weekend, Melody had accompanied her Aunt Pansy to the Bergen Mall in Paramus, New Jersey and was awestruck by the beautiful foliage. The leaves on the trees displayed a rainbow of colors: gold, red, orange and brown. "No wonder New Jersey is called the Garden State," she had thought.

Mi Neva Know Sey

Melody is on her way to school alone, because Roderick is sick with a bad cold. "Hope me don't get sick like Roddy, because me drinking the cold bush tea to keep my resistance strong. No sah, I don't want to catch any pneumonia," Melody says to herself.

When she arrives at school, she notices that Ariel is absent. She later learns that Ariel is also out with the flu. Many of her classmates are absent for the same reason. However, Melody takes special note of the continued absence of one classmate. Debbie Smith is out again, for the third week in a row. Melody is really concerned about Debbie, especially after overhearing Debbie's mother's conversation with Mrs. Varma on conference night.

"Something must be wrong! I wonder what?" Melody muses. She is still thinking about Debbie when she meets Kirk in the cafeteria for lunch.

"Give me a break! This hamburger tastes like rubber. Is wha this dem give us to eat, today, man?", Melody exclaims, while forcing herself to finish her hamburger.

"You are so right, Melody, and you said it just right. Blimey, this does taste like a piece of rubber!" Kirk is in full agreement.

When Melody hears the mention of Debbie Smith's name, her attention is drawn to the two girls at the table in front of them. Her ears stand on alert, as she tries to eavesdrop on their conversation. She recognizes one of the girls as Cherie Tucker, from her class. Although the girls are obviously trying to speak quietly, their voices are clear to Melody.

"Yea, girl, she sure is pregnant. Two months, I heard," says Cherie's lunch mate.

"Ain't Debbie only thirteen," asks Cherie.

"Well, almost fourteen. Next month, I b'leve."

"So, who is the Daddy, Latoya?"

"I don't remember his name, Cherie. But ah know him though. He be in high school, with my sister Tanya. Yep, he a freshman."

"Get outta here, Latoya. You kidding me, right? A high school brother!"

"Huh, huh! "Bout fifteen or sixteen years old."

"Guess Mrs. Varma knows by now."

"Should," Latoya responds, obliviously.

Melody and Kirk had heard enough for Melody to identify the Debbie of the girl's conversation as Debbie Smith, her classmate. Her suspicions are now confirmed. She puts it all together: Debbie's constant sleeping in class, her mother's concern and her absence. Instead of gloating, Melody feels sorry for Debbie, who is only thirteen years old and about to become a mother.

"She is only a kid like myself," she says, more to herself, than to Kirk.

* * * * * *

Melody does not remember teenage pregnancy being a major problem in Jamaica when she lived there. At least, she does not recall any thirteen-year-old that she knew being pregnant. Yet, she would be the first to admit that she did not know everyone in the country, and the possibility exists that young children could have gotten pregnant.

She recalls that when she was ten, Greta, a fourteen-year-old friend, who lived next door to her, told her about the 'birds and the beasts. At least, that was the way Greta put it, referring to sex education. Grannyma was unaware of her granddaughter's early sex education, until the day she sat her down, and counseled her about puberty. Melody had just turned twelve.

"How you mean, you know," inquired Grannyma.

"I . . . I mean, yes, Grannyma. I know. I understand what you talking about. I don't know nothing about anything, mam."

"Listen here, gal pickney. Is you friend telling you dem things the wrong way, nuh? Don't listen to what nobody else tell you. Just listen to what I say to you."

Grannyma had taken a sip of hot chocolate from her big white mug and continued. "All mi telling you, Miss Melody, is that you are twelve now, soon turn teenager, and Massa God going to make your body change into a woman. Just be careful around boys."

Melody had hung her head down, looking at the floor, while her grandmother gave her counsel.

"You hear me? Look up at me, little girl, when I talking to you. Yuh Mammy not here to tell you all of this, but I am telling you. You getting big now. You turning into a woman."

"Yes, Grannyma. Ah listening, mam."

Mi Neva Know Sey

When her grandmother had finished, Melody had not learned anything new. She had only heard it said differently from the way Greta had related it to her. Greta had embellished her lesson with a story she had heard, which was passed down by a few people in the district. The story was about a fourteen-year-old schoolgirl in the district, who became pregnant and shocked the entire town. Back then; the girl's family was reproached by the whole neighborhood. Greta had related the story while they were sitting under the big mango tree on a moonshine night.

"Is lie you telling, Greta. No fourteen-year-old can't have no baby. Only big woman. Go weh!" Melody said to Greta.

"Lawkes, man! Melody, how come you so fool, fool. You stupid, eeh, man. Of course children can have baby. You a little pickney feh true. You see from you turn twelve, you can have baby, man."

Melody, at ten, still found Greta's story hard to believe but, since Greta was older, she trusted her. So Greta had continued the tale of one Adina Johnson, who became pregnant and had to leave school and stayed locked up in her mother's house most of the time.

"Mi hear seh, you nuh, that Adina never come out of har mother house, atall. And a whole heap a times, people, mostly her school friends, used to pass the yard and stop to see her big belly." Greta paused and held her stomach and laughed.

"Mi seh, Melody, dem time, that was a big big thing feh happen in the district, you nuh. So now, mi hear seh, when the school pickney stop feh peep on Adina, her mother used to come out and cuss them off and tell them feh mind dem own business. She tell them seh, 'What sweet nanny goat now a go run him belly, later.'" Greta laughed again, holding her stomach. "Then, hear the sweet part now, Mel. The mother take a pan of water and throw 'pon the fase pickney dem, and dem run."

Melody had listened with interest and sympathy to the story. When her friend finished, she said, quite innocently, "Me not getting pregnant when me little, atall. Me no want feel so shame and make people look pon me."

* * * * * *

As Melody and Kirk finish their lunch and leave the cafeteria, the bad taste left by the hamburger was not the only unpalatable taste in their mouths. They now had the bad news about their classmate's pregnancy to contemplate. The fact that they were from different cultures -- Jamaica and England – made this a whole new experience to them. And, for Melody, this was just another item to add to her growing list of "Mi never know seh" experiences.

As the days pass by and Melody thinks about her classmate becoming a mother and raising a baby, she cannot help but contemplate how Debbie's future will be altered. She wonders if Debbie will ever finish school. After all, she is only fourteen and not even in high school yet.

Melody is determined to investigate how problems like these are handled in America. Although she did not know too much about social issues in Jamaica, she is almost sure that once a schoolgirl, young or old, had a baby, she was on her own. But something tells her it is not so in America. No! not America. America provides for its people. She already knows about the welfare system, as many of her schoolmates are recipients and tell her all about the schemes. Sure enough, her assumptions about the provisions for pregnant teenagers are confirmed by her teacher, Mrs. Varma.

"Oh yes, Melody, we have a special school for girls like Debbie. Pregnant students are given the opportunity to attend classes until they give birth. And they can return to school, later, if they so desire."

"That is so good to know, Mrs. Varma." This knowledge, in essence, takes a weight off Melody's shoulders. It is difficult to explain why she is so concerned about Debbie, but her concerns are natural.

Her teacher eyes her cautiously.

"No! No! Miss. Not me, no way! I am just curious, Miss. I know you know about Debbie by now."

"Yes, I do. Her mother called me the day she found out," Mrs. Varma says with a sigh. "It is sad that these young girls are not more careful. And, usually, when one baby comes, then a second and third follow. Melody you are a beautiful girl and smart too. I can only encourage you, as your teacher, to be very careful."

"Yes, Miss. I will be. Thanks, Mrs. Varma."

"You know, sometimes I wonder if the resources we have to meet these problems are more of an attraction and bait which, in the long run, contribute to the problem." Mrs. Varma shuffles in her chair, feeling a bit uneasy having this discussion with her student. "Oh, yes, Melody, take for instance this program that Debbie can enroll in, EMIS."

"What you say, Mrs. Varma, Emis?"

"EMIS stands for Expectant Mothers In School. This is a regular classroom set up with teachers like me, Melody. The expecting girls are schooled by the same curriculum as in a regular Public School. All they have do is to show up, if they want to get an education."

"That is really nice. Well, I mean that is nice that the government cares that much to do this. They are lucky, I believe, and they should appreciate it."

"Exactly, Melody. It is good to talk to someone like you. You are only thirteen, but you think quite maturely. You kids these days (not you, in particular, but kids, in general) have a whole lot at your fingertips. Sometimes, it just seems to me that because the services are available, kids do whatever they want to do, because they know there is a solution to their errors."

"Uh, huh." Melody says, listening quite attentively. "I know what you mean, Mrs. Varma. We don't have this kind of program back in Jamaica, mam. And if a girl drops out of school and she really wants to get an education, she has to find a school on her own. I don't remember any of my friends or anybody getting pregnant at my age when I was in Jamaica," she says, rubbing her forehead, "but I heard that if it happens, the girls go back to Commercial School or Secretarial Business School on their own."

"I see. Sounds like in my days, when I was growing up." Mrs. Varma looks at her watch to see the time. "Time is going, Melody. But back in my days, young girls behaved and kept themselves well. At least, the majority of them did. See, I was born and raised down south, in a little town called Cayton, in South Carolina. My Mama raised six girls and one boy -- yea, he was so spoiled then, I coulda thrown him out," she laughs. "Yep, we six girls never had any babies 'til we all were married. We married young, but we did the right thing. Only eighteen when I married Jake, my husband. Good old JV, they used to call him. Jacob Varma. We had four of our own, and we are still married.

"Like I said, we tried not to mess around and get ourselves pregnant until it was the right time. If we did, we paid for it in a whole lot a ways. Well, Melody it was sure nice talking to you. Now run along, and don't you spend too much time worrying about little Miss Debbie. She'll be alright."

Melody has learned so much from Mrs. Varma. She realizes that if there is a school, the EMIS for pregnant girls, then school pregnancy is not a new problem. It is an old problem that is already being addressed. Only a country like America, she thinks, can do this.

"It a'right, still you know. School children still get the chance to clean up dem lives, even when they make mistakes, and nothing wrong with that. But me still agree with Miss, that some time the system can spoil people."

She repeats the line of the pledge, "With liberty and justice for all." Truly, she admits America is a land of liberty. A land of opportunity and the reason why many people seek to be part of its promise. No wonder the saying, "God bless America," is so often used.

A Wonderful American Experience

The month of November seems to be disappearing extremely fast. It is already the last week, and school is hectic as usual. Classrooms and hallways in school are brightly decorated with drawings and pictures for Thanksgiving Day. In some of the classrooms and the auditorium, there are captions and illustrations commemorating one of America's biggest holiday celebrations. Melody has already been educated on the significance of this holiday by her brother, television commercials and her Social Studies class.

Celebrated on the last Thursday in November, Thanksgiving Day is one of America's biggest family holidays, followed by Christmas and New Year's Day. Melody has experienced several traditional holidays since she arrived in America in early summer. Her first experience was Fourth of July, America's Independence Day. That was exciting. Fourth of July brought the experience of barbecues and fireworks. Melody enjoyed herself at the home of one of her mother's friends from work, an American woman, who went all out in celebration of this holiday.

She did not enjoy Labor Day that much. Labor Day is celebrated on the first Monday in September, *a few days* before school reopens. To Melody, it was similar to the 4th of July, but her family joined some of their relatives, along with her mother's friend, in a big cookout at a large park. Labor Day actually closes out the summer and she watched the parade on television. But no amount of fun could have relieved the jitters and preoccupation Melody felt about attending school for the first time in America, she now admits. Halloween was next and she hated that festival. Now, here comes Thanksgiving Day, which she has heard so much about. She is looking forward to this holiday. Certainly, for the past two weeks, she has learned a great deal about the history behind Thanksgiving Day, and has come to appreciate it.

She has one thing in mind for which to give special thanks, although it may seem trivial and insignificant to others. It is the fact that she has not had a problem with Wanda, her schoolmate, recently. "Thank you, Lord," says Melody. "From the day I stand up to her in the bathroom, she hasn't bothered me again."

Three days before Thanksgiving, Melody is again consoled that Wanda seems to be no longer a problem. "Wanda . . . my . . . my (she cannot find the right adjective to describe her), 'sensey fowl' is staying out of my way; is a good blessing to be thankful for." She smiles, cunningly, as she recalls how vicious these types of fowls were in Jamaica.

By Wednesday, Melody has more to be thankful for. On her way to school, that morning, she is full of glee. "Yipee! Half a day, today, then two days off from school, well, actually four days, if you count the weekend. For this I give you thanks, Jesus."

Roderick does not hear her shout of jubilation. It is in the form of one of her silent conversations with herself. Furthermore, Roderick is not his usual self this morning. He is very unhappy and is quiet, which is quite unusual. Melody is aware of his sadness and knows why. She is amused by the situation, but is cautious not to be obvious about her amusement.

"Come on, Roderick, man. You don't look goofy, as you call it, atall. You look cute in you Pilgrim outfit, man."

"Don't try to let me feel good, Mel. Yea, it is easy for you to say, for you don't got to wear it."

"I am not lying. For real, Roddy. You do look cute."

"Mel. Stop! Stop teasing me," he says, stomping his foot on the ground. "Today, I feel the same way you felt about wearing a Halloween costume. Remember? Only, I got to wear this costume or I lose points in my Social Studies class."

Roderick is really upset. Melody stops being conciliatory towards him. She admits that he does have a point about her attitude toward Halloween. She shrugs her shoulders and thinks, "Cho, that different. This costume is for learning and understanding all about Thanksgiving."

Roderick ignores her as he walks the rest of the way to school in an absentminded trance.

Melody learns that in school the students in the lower grades are given a thorough background about the history of Thanksgiving. To help them understand the history, practical application is made to facilitate their learning about the early settlers in America. Thanksgiving is traced back to the Pilgrims, as these early settlers were called. They traveled by ship, The Mayflower, to America, from England, via the Netherlands. The journey commenced around 1607, in order to escape religious persecution. Upon their arrival in America, their ship docked at Plymouth, Massachusetts. Many of the new settlers died from the cold and diseases, but those who survived gave thanks and celebrated the first Thanksgiving feast with the Indian natives. Corn, fish and turkey were the main food provisions, along with other harvested crops, used in the celebration. Since then, Thanksgiving Day has become an American tradition.

When Roderick and Melody arrive at his school, she notices several other "Pilgrims" running around the schoolyard. From the look on his face, Melody can tell that Roderick still feels shy and embarrassed in his outfit.

"Hey, Roderick! Over here, come on," Roderick's friend Dante calls out to him.

"I am okay. I don't feel like playing, today," Roderick replies to his friend.

"Hey, you look cool," Dante compliments Roderick on his outfit.

"Yea, right, Dante. Don't you feel stupid in these hats?"

"Nah, everybody knows it is for the play. Shoo. It ain't bother me none."

Roderick finally relaxes and walks over to play catch with his friends. Melody, who had kept an eye on her brother, smiles. Leave it to Dante to get Roderick out of his funk, she thinks.

Melody continues around the block to her school, amused by her brother's action. Roderick and his friends play a game of catch until the bell rings for the students to march in.

In this particular school district, The Board of Education has set up a special co-op learning relationship between the Elementary and Junior High school. This allows both schools to share in special events. The morning's agenda for the Junior High is, General Assembly, in the auditorium. Melody has attended a few of these assemblies before, but they were lectures from outside professionals. Once, representatives from the New York Police Department visited and talked about the danger of drugs. Today's assembly will consist of entertainment by a group of students from the Elementary School. Grades Seven and Eight will be entertained by their neighboring school.

After the pledge of allegiance is said, and attendance is taken in the classrooms, the teachers and the hall monitors work together to get the classes seated quietly in the auditorium. Melody's class is the last to enter. She is right behind Mrs. Wolmer's Seventh Grade class. And, for the first time, Melody finds out that her antagonist, Wanda, is in a lower grade than she is in. She is surprised.

"Eh, eh! She only in Seventh Grade. That deh big ole girl. Mi sure seh she is my age or even older."

Ariel sees her staring at Wanda and reads her mind. In an attempted whisper, she says to Melody, "Caramba!"

Melody knows this word now and responds to Ariel's surprise.

"She in Seventh Grade, only!"

"Uh! Huh!" Brooke, who is standing right behind Melody and Ariel, offers a response. "Yep. She thinks she is Miss "Bully" Wanda. Got left back in Seventh Grade. Suspended many times."

Melody says nothing, but assumes a look of surprise, lips folded and eyes widened. In the auditorium, Melody sits flanked by Ariel and Brooke. She likes Brooke a lot and being friends with her, has made her aware that not all American girls are like Wanda. Brooke is also very smart and is of help to Melody from time to time with her schoolwork.

The selected group of students from the primary grades are already seated in the auditorium, and Roderick is among them. They are going to perform a Thanksgiving play "Let us all be quiet now. Everyone. We are about to begin," announces Vice Principal Josephine Griffith, attempting to be heard over the noise. "Today, we, that is, the staff and the intermediate grades, will be entertained and, at the same time, educated and reminded, what Thanksgiving is all about. Please try to be very attentive and supportive to our actors, from our primary grades." She points to them sitting in front. "Let them feel good, especially those of you who have brothers and sisters in these grades. Let us all put our hands together and give them a big round of applause."

A roaring ovation is heard throughout the auditorium, along with muffled sounds of whistling and booing from the older boys. The performing classes go on stage. The performers include boys and girls of all heights, shapes and nationality. The boys are dressed in big brown and black bowl hats and the girls are dressed in long dresses with aprons. The stage setting vividly portrays the Pilgrim's lifestyle and culture. Most of the performers appear excited.

When the play is over, the audience cheers. Roderick too, is smiling. He had been a little embarrassed by the earlier booing of the older boys, but became more relaxed on stage with his fellow actors. His eyes meet his sister's and they both smile, as Melody quietly forms the words with lips, "Very good Roderick."

The entire school, present in the auditorium, stands and sings a favorite Thanksgiving song.

"Happy Thanksgiving. Be safe, and see you next week," says Vice Principal Griffith, as she raps up her closing remarks and dismisses school for the day. There is great rumbling as the students disperse from the room.

"Hab a Happy Thanksgiving, Melody. Hope you like your first Thanksgiving in America."

"You, too, Ariel. You staying home?"

"No. I go wid mi familia to Passaic, New Hersey (Jersey) to my cousins for big celebration. How about you?"

"Oh. I am staying right here in Brooklyn, but we are having people over to our house. A whole lot of my family will be there."

"Well, enjoy. See you next week, Melody. Goodbye, Brooke. Enjoy!"

There seems to be a lot of activity in the streets, with people shopping and preparing for Thanksgiving Day. By the time Melody arrives home, she is very sleepy, but instead of going to bed, she decides to watch a soap opera on television. During the summer, before she started school, when she had just arrived in America, she had watched all the daytime shows and still continues to watch them when she gets a chance. Her favorite is "One Life to Live". She has come to realize that regardless of the amount of time that elapses between watching the soaps, as soon as she watches them again, she picks up the story, as if she had never stopped watching.

She now sits in front of the television with a piece of bun and cheese and a glass of milk and stays there until "One Life to Live" ends. Her mother, meanwhile, is watching another show, "As the World Turns," on another TV station, while in the kitchen, preparing dinner before, she goes to work.

Mrs. Pennycook has requested the day off on Thanksgiving, since she will be hosting a large family gathering this year. There are many chores to be done before the big day and she needs her daughters' help. "Thank God, Mel come home early today," Mrs. Pennycook says, to herself.

"Miss Mel, come here putus," she calls to Melody from the kitchen. She takes pleasure in addressing her daughters with various nicknames.

"Coming, Mama." Melody had dozed off and had barely heard her mother's summons. "Yes, mam," she yawns wearily as she enters the kitchen.

"What! You was sleeping? But stop. Anyway, I want you and Bubbles to do some things later so that we don't have too much to do for tomorrow."

"Yes, Mama. What?"

Her mother gives her a list of all the things that she and Bubbles should do, including cutting up and juicing the coconut for the rice and peas.

"All right, Mama, we will do everything."

Melody does not mind cutting up the coconut to be juiced in the electric blender. In Jamaica, she had hated grating the coconut with the aluminum grater. She used to waste Grannyma's coconut because she never waited until the coconut was grated down too far for fear of cutting her hand.

* * * * * *

When Bubbles comes home later, she is exhausted because after school (which was dismissed early) she accompanied her friend, Arice, into Manhattan. The trip for them was only for fun and to browse in some of the big department stores, like Saks Fifth Ave. She goes right to her room, drops her book bag on the floor and collapses on her bed.

"Lawkes, ah tired yuh see," she says out loud to herself, unaware that Melody is standing at the door.

"You should be. Look how long school let out and is now you just coming home," Melody reprimands her sister.

"Lawkes, Melody, man! You frighten me, yuh know. Please do! Give me a few minutes, fun nice, but it tiresome sometimes. Is all the way up Manhattan me coming from. Bwoy, them subway train noisy, and just to look at some of them people mek mi feel exhausted. Good thing no school for the rest of the week." Bubbles slumps backwards on her bed and puts the pillow over her face.

"Excuse me, my dear, you see this?" Melody waves a piece of paper in the air. "This is the list of things Mama wants us to do this evening. So rest a while Miss happy-go-lucky, but we can't let Mama down; moreover I am so excited about this Thanksgiving."

"Tonight?" Bubbles hisses her teeth and sits up in the bed. "What we have to do?"

"It's all here, my dear big sister, the paper will be right on the fridge when you are ready."

Melody walks back to the living room and does not see the cut eye (nasty look) Bubbles gives her. An hour later, Bubbles walks into the kitchen yawning and prepares something to eat before she begins her chores. Melody is already doing some of hers and, after Bubbles is finished eating, she checks the list and begins her part of the holiday preparations. The sisters engage in a friendly conversation as they work.

"Mi seh, Melody, the store mi go to, today, pretty and big yuh see. Is there me want to work for summer."

"Which store. What's the name?"

"Saks."

"Really! Me always see them advertise in the paper."

"Listen to this, Mel. Mi friend Arice, no easy. Mi seh the girl try out about ten different perfumes. I can't tell you what she smell like, when she finished."

Melody and Bubbles laugh heartily and are surprised that they have finished all they had to do, so quickly. Bubbles looks at her sister after she has finished cutting up the colored greens and smiles. "I am done, thank God. Time really flies when you talk and work."

The sisters take a second look at the list, to make sure all the tasks are done. A feeling of oneness overshadows them and they experience a special bond. Deep in their hearts is the joy of being in America with their family, as they look forward to their first Thanksgiving celebration. After all the chores are done, Bubbles, Melody and Roderick watch a movie on television until 10:30 p.m. For another half an hour, they channel hop, trying to find something else interesting to watch, but with no luck. Bubbles and Melody decide to watch the news on the ABC station, although Roderick tries to talk them out of it. "Shu," he mutters. "This is boring."

He gets up to leave the room, but Melody playfully pulls him back to the couch.

It is almost 11:30 p.m. and, since their mother will be home soon, they decide to wait up for her. She can't complain, they decide, since there is no school the next day and all the chores have been completed. They are all excited about Thanksgiving. Aunt Pansy and family; their Dad's sister, Pearl, and her family from Canada, other relatives and friends will be visiting them on this special day.

"Unoo wait up all night for me?" Mrs. Pennycook greets her three children, as she walks in the door. "I still have some work to do before I go to bed. Any of you want to help?" she asks, already knowing what their response will be.

"No, Mama," they reply in unison.

"We jus' wanted to make sure you come home safe, Mama. Mi tired, though," Melody says, rubbing her eyes.

"Thank you. Good night!" Mrs. Pennycook gives each a hug, then sets about doing her chores. She cooks the red peas and prepares some other dishes that can be cooked overnight. He sister, Pansy will bring the potato salad, carrot salad, the carrot juice and a pork roast, as planned. She drinks a cup of mint tea and then retires to bed.

* * * * * *

The doorbell rings at 6:00 a.m. Mr. Pennycook opens the door and greets his sister Pearl, his brother-in-law Derrick, his two nieces, Donita and Davina, and his nephew Dalton. They are tired and sleepy from the long journey to New York from Toronto. The children go immediately to their cousins' rooms to catch up on the rest of their sleep. Derrick, and Pearl chat with Winston for a while before retiring to bed.

Mrs. Pennycook is still asleep, after having gone to bed at about 1:00 a.m. "I want to get up about 8:00 o'clock in the morning," she warned her husband. "So when Pearlie and Derrick come, don't wake me. Just show them where them going to sleep."

At 7:30 a.m., the telephone rings, waking up Mrs. Pennycook. She had forgotten to turn off the ringer on the phone in her bedroom. "Hello!" she says, drowsily, into the phone. "Who?"

"Is me, Lurline. Noel lost the directions Winston gave us the other day. Can I have it again?"

Lurline is her cousin who lives in Connecticut. She is also due at the Pennycooks for Thanksgiving dinner.

"Cho, man, Lurline! Me just trying to get a little last minute sleep. Went to bed late last night. Well, this morning, actually. Mek Noel so careless, man. See Winston here."

She hands her husband the phone. He attempts to give the directions to Lurline, who is having a hard time following him. "Yes, take 95 South to New York. Right!" He is silent. "Yes, Lurline, take the Throgs Neck Bridge, not the George Washington Bridge. Otherwise, you will end up in Jersey."

He repeats the direction about three times before he hangs up. Mrs. Pennycook, who is lying beside him, is annoyed. She eventually decides to forego sleep and gets up to go to the bathroom. On the way to the bathroom, she stumbles over the suitcases in the hallway.

"Lawkes, man! That Winston, you see. Can't depend 'pon him to do anything. Mi beg him to put him sister and her family things in the room and him leave dem right here. Cho, man!"

Anel yawns while she washes her face. She decides to take a quick shower, then returns to her room to get dressed. "Might as well mi get up. I have a long day ahead of me. These get-togethers are fun, but Lord, too much work," she mumbles to herself as she dresses.

She then heads to the kitchen and starts preparing breakfast for her sister-in-law and her family, as well as Winston and the children. Liver, green banana, yellow yam and, a big fresh hard dough bread is on the breakfast menu. It will be a special breakfast, since it is not too often that the family has the opportunity to eat together.

The day has just begun. The best is yet to come. Anel is looking forward to a great time with all her family and friends on this special Thanksgiving Day.

Melody is awakened by the smell of the sauteed liver her mother is preparing. She sees her cousins sleeping soundly in Bubbles' bed. She, too, is looking forward to her first Thanksgiving Day in America. Already she believes she will have a great time.

* * * * * *

By 2:30 p.m., all the Pennycooks' guests have arrived. The house is full of chatter and laughter. Mrs. Pennycook's sister Pansy, her husband Riccardo, and their children, Delraya and Ricky Junior, are the last ones to arrive, although they live the closet. Lurline and Noel finally arrived from Connecticut, exhausted. They had missed one of the exits and had gone out of their way. When they arrived, Winston detected immediately that Lurline had some difficulty with the directions, due to the distressed look on her face.

Geraldine Jones, a good friend of Anel's, has made herself at home and is enjoying some of the Jamaican goodies (hors d'oeurves) Anel has prepared. Dinner is finally ready and the table is filled with a variety of dishes. The golden-roasted, 20 pound-Butterball turkey is sitting in the middle of the table; the glazed ham, decorated with pineapple topping, is next to it. The curried goat, roast pork, rice and peas, collard greens and steamed cabbage, with carrots send out a mouthwatering aroma. The other traditional Thanksgiving trimmings, cranberry sauce, Mrs. Pennycooks' homemade stuffing and candied yams, add to the grand display of dishes.

Beverages include carrot juice, sorrell and fruit punch. For dessert, Pansy brought three sweet potato pies and two apple pies. A small rum fruitcake is also one of the dessert treats.

Melody cannot believe her eyes. She has never seen so much food in one place for the number of people present. The only thing she can compare this occasion to, is a "nine night" she had attended when she was about ten years old. She recalls that Grannyma's eighty-year-old cousin, Zach, had died and a big feast was held nine days after his death. His widow, Miss Rachel, killed three goats and there was food galore, and the entire district was there to have a bellyful.

Melody smiles as she recalls how she was afraid to go to the nine-night because she was apprehensive of cousin Zach's duppy. The festivities of that night are still fresh in her mind. Many people danced, and sang, and some of the men and older women drank plenty of the free Red Stripe beer, and white rum Miss Rachel supplied. Melody had fallen asleep on the sofa in the living room as morning approached, and when she woke up later, she was in her own bed.

She looks at the food in front of her now and thinks to herself, "No wonder today name Thanksgiving Day. This amount of food is enough to give thanks for."

The family gathers around the table for dinner, which is being served buffet style.

Winston turns to his brother-in-law, "Oh, Brother Deacon please to bless the table, Sir."

Derrick D'Costa is deacon in his church, The Faith Holiness Assembly, in Toronto. He prays a long prayer and stops only when his wife gives him a nudge. When the blessing of the food ends, Roderick and his cousin Dalton are the first to help themselves to a plate.

"Hold on, young boys. Let the older ones go first," Mr. Pennycook reproves them. "And first let me carve big Mr. Turkey here."

"Oh, can I have one of the drumsticks, please, Dad," Roderick calls out to his father.

"Me, too, Uncle Winston, please," Dalton puts in his order, right after his cousin.

Mr. Pennycook uses a sharp knife and carves several slices of the bird for the first serving. He hands one drumstick to the each boy. "Young fellows, hold your plates. Here you go."

All of the guests and family members help themselves to a hearty serving, but just enough to start them off. They realize there is plenty of food and do not want to start off with too much. Melody is the last to make a plate and she decides to take a little bit of all the food she likes first. She takes a couple slices of turkey with some gravy and hesitates about taking any of the cranberry sauce, but then takes a small bit to taste it. She then takes a seat next to her Aunt Pearl and begins to eat.

"Umm! The turkey a'right, kinda taste like chicken," Melody thinks. She puts a piece of the cranberry sauce, in her mouth. "This taste tangy sweetish. Reminds me of guava jam and jello, too." She is not too crazy about the sauce but she finishes the amount on her plate.

The room is semi-quiet. Everyone is eating, and only make muffled responses because their mouths are full. The atmosphere is hushed. Halfway through the meal, the men start talking about any subject that comes to mind. Sports, politics and religion. The women talk about nothing in particular to the person next to them.

Melody listens and responds occasionally to any questions directed to her.

"So, Melody, how you like America so far?" inquires her cousin Lurline.

"I like it, cousin Lurline."

"You don't sound too sure, though."

"Well . . . cousin Lurline, right now, I don't like the cold weather, mam."

"Nobody does mi child. But you will get use to it. And sometimes you will freeze, but you won't die."

"I hope not," Melody smiles.

She eats some of the candied yam. She loves it. It is made of American yam,(a type of sweet potato), covered over with Karo syrup and marshmallow topping. Melody had watched as, her mother prepared it, using the recipe she got from her friend at work. She likes it and intends to get another helping.

"So, hope you adjusted to your new school by now. You like it, right?" Lurline continues to throw questions at her.

Melody rolls her eyes upward, pensively, and hesitates before replying to Lurline's question. She then glances over to where her mother is sitting, but her mother deliberately looks away.

"Tell you the truth, cousin Lurline, school is very different over here. No uniforms in the public school where I go. Mi would rather wear uniform, mam."

"Ah know what you mean child. Noel been going to school here since Kindergarten. Thank God him only have one year left in high school."

Her cousin Noel was born in America and lived in New York before the family moved to Connecticut.

"One thing I must advise you, though, Melody, honey, is to study your lesson and be the best. Stay out of the wrong company. It not easy, 'cause 'Merica have everything and pickney can get spoil easy."

"Yes, mam."

"And you are a pretty little girl, young teenager . . . and when you start getting bigger, the boys them will want to come after you . . . ," she stops short, interrupted by Pansy, Melody's aunt.

"Come on, Lurline, man, stop asking the little girl so much questions. Give her time to breathe. Cho, leave me niece alone."

"Stop you noise, Pansy. Is jealous yuh jealous. I just finding out how mi beautiful little cousin doing in America. 'Cause the last time mi see her was a long time ago when I went down to Jamaica."

They all laugh hilariously at Lurline's and Pansy's amusing bickering, as this is the way the two relatives always act when they are together.

Everyone has taken second and third servings, including the dessert. They are full and sleepy. Mrs. Pennycook cannot sit still, and is busy moving around and talking to her family at the same time.

Eh eh! niggeritis has taken over," she gestures toward Winston and Derrick, who are trying to fight off the sleep, which is creeping up on them.

Melody giggles to herself. She knows what her mother means when she refers to niggeritis. It is a made up idiom for the bad habit of wanting or going to sleep after eating. She believes it is an accurate saying for the present situation, because she too is feeling drowsy. She looks quickly around the room to see what the others are doing. Bubbles and Delraya are deep in conversation. Noel and Ricky Junior seem to be having an interesting chat also, and her Canadian cousins and their Mom are talking while watching television. Geraldine, her mother's co-worker, left early, because she has to work later and needs to catch up on her sleep. Riccardo and Pansy are sitting together, doing nothing in particular. Lurline is helping Mrs. Pennycook clean up the table and put the leftovers away. And only God knows what Roderick and Dalton are up to! They are nowhere in sight.

Melody leaves them all, and quietly retires to her room. She wants to be alone. A sudden surge of emptiness has overtaken her, and she is not sure if it is a result of her being so stuffed and sleepy. She stretches out on her back on the bed, closes her eyes and reflects on Jamaica. Her grandmother and her friend Retinella are in her thoughts and she wishes they could be here on this special Thanksgiving Day. She also thinks of most of the people in the district back in Jamaica, especially the families with many children and all those mouths to feed.

"Look how much food we have tonight. Mama don't have to cook for another two days, with all the leftovers," she sighs. "Lord, I hope they have food to eat right now. I hope everybody has food to eat like us."

Her eyes are still closed, and she feels warm teardrops trickling down the side of her face. She whispers her favorite line: "Me never know sey," and again repeats it. "Mi never know sey me would feel so mix up in mi mind in America. I am happy right now. Mi having a good time with mi family. But mi feel sad and worried about mi friends in Jamaica."

Thanksgiving Day was a wonderful experience. Melody enjoyed it all. She promises herself that over the weekend she will do some physical work around the house to burn up some of the calories. And, of course, she will have to write to Retinella and tell her about this special day.

She soon falls asleep as she sits thinking about Jamaica. When she awakens, three hours later, she finds the house very quiet and still. Those who had to leave are already gone and those who remained are sound asleep. She brushes her teeth, get dressed for bed and goes back to sleep.

* * * * * *

On Friday, Melody does some house chores, as she had promised herself, then goes to the Library with her cousins, Donita and Davina. Later, in the evening, Mr. Pennycook takes his nieces, nephew, and children bowling. The family enjoys a couple of games; females against males. On their way home, Roderick and Dalton, are still beaming over their victory against their sisters.

The next morning, Saturday, as Melody awakens, she hears loud chattering and laughter coming from the kitchen. She yawns lazily as she alights from the bed. The delicious smell of breakfast travels from the kitchen to her bedroom.

"Good morning, Mama and Dada. Good morning, Auntie Pearl and Uncle Derrick, Melody says as she walks into the kitchen, still rubbing the sleep from her eyes.

"Good morning, Mel, sweetheart," they all reply in unison.

"Mel, Mel, since you up, you want to come to New Jersey with us?" her dad asks.

"Who going to New Jersey and why? When Auntie them leaving?"

"As soon as we finished eating, mi child. We leaving now so I can stop in New Jersey to do a little shopping, and Winston coming with us." Pearl munches on a fried dumpling, as she explains to Melody.

"Ahoa! All right, me will come then. Maybe I can find a dress for next month's trip to Washington, D.C."

"You going to Washington, DC. What for?" Pearl is curious.

"Oh yes, my dear sister-in law. My Melody was selected to represent her school in a writing contest, Anel explains, proudly. They call it writing simp-something. What it name, Melody?"

"Symposium, Mama."

"Is what you saying to mi, Anel! That is really nice. I am proud of you, Melody."

Melody blushes at being the center of attention, and excuses herself to get ready to leave with her dad.

Soon, everyone is ready to pull out and head for New Jersey. Melody loves going to New Jersey. She has been there several times before. It is less jumbled and less busy than Brooklyn and New York City, as a whole. When she first traveled to New Jersey, she agreed that calling it the Garden State was appropriate.

At the Burlington Coat factory on Route 17 in Paramus, they find bargains galore. Melody finds a beautiful black evening dress, at a reasonable price, for her upcoming event. A rush of excitement passes over her as she thinks about her upcoming trip. In Jamaica, she had never been selected to represent her school in such a manner. The only experience she had had in Jamaica was a class trip to Castleton Gardens, in Upper St. Andrews, and it could not be compared to her upcoming trip to Washington, D.C.

"Mi never know sey mi would turn big shot in America so quick! Bwoy, mi kan't lie. Me like this part feh true," she now admits to herself. She is still rummaging through the dress rack, deep in thought, while looking at other dresses, when her father startles her.

"Melody, we ready; are you?"

"Yes, Dada."

The DaCostas say their goodbyes as they leave the Pennycooks for their long journey back to Toronto, Ontario. Mr. Pennycook and Melody drive back to Brooklyn.

Church No Problem

The temperature on Sunday morning is only 20 degrees. Melody is lazy to get out of bed to go to church, but gets up anyway. She has been lackadaisical about going to church every Sunday, since the winter started. But since she has been off from school since Wednesday, she knows she will feel guilty if she stays home.

"At least it is not snowing," she acknowledges. "And the church warm."

She has been going to church regularly since late summer, except for a few times when she could not make it. Melody had always loved going to church back home in Spanish Town with her grandmother. Grannyma is a born again, saved and sanctified, in-good-standing Christian church mother. She is a faithful disciple of the Good Shepherd Apostolic Holiness Church, which is located ten miles from her home. Although Melody can only recall her early church-going days as far back as the age of five, she was informed by her grandmother that she had been christened in the same church. She had just turned a year old when she was blessed by Pastor Lattibeaudere.

Grannyma had related the christening story to a then, seven-year-old Melody, one Sunday morning, as she combed her hair for Sunday School. "You mama, didn't want to come with me to church that morning. Say me alone fe go this time, causing say she shame since is the second time she mek mistake. But I told her right to her face that it would only be nine-day talk when the people dem see her."

As Grannyma combed Melody's long hair, she occasionally tugged on it to pull her closer: "Mel, keep you head still, so that ah can get fe handle mi hand good. You know seh ah can't manage this a head of hair too easy. Anyway, as I was saying, I insist that you mother come to take part in your blessing, 'cause she did it for Bubbles and she must do it for you, too."

Grannyma had continued her story, in all seriousness, relating it as if the incident had just recently occurred.

"Mi know seh is fraide, fraide, she did fraide, fraide because yuh look much different from yuh sister. Aye sah! What really hurt me, is that Anel really never show up that morning. And when she come fe see me later, ah told her don't even bodder to tell me why, causing seh no excuse could suit me. Today, I can only thank Massa Jesus that Him change mi heart so that ah don't keep hatred locked up inside."

Melody remembers the story of her first time in church well, and is convinced that her relationship with her grandmother had contributed to her love for church, at least up until about the age of nine. She had particularly enjoyed Sunday School, regular services and the special revival services. When she had turned ten, her enthusiasm had diminished, but she continued going anyway. Attending church had become a part of her routine. Sometimes, she hated going because of the length of the services. Grannyma did not tolerate her sleeping in church, at that age, as she had done when she was younger.

After Sunday School, which lasted an hour, from 11:00 a.m. to 12.00 p.m., the afternoon service began at 12.30 p.m. and continued until about 3:00 p.m. or later. Even now as she recalls; she frowns, remembering how her stomach growled when she was hungry.

Still, the worst part about going to church in Jamaica, was getting there. The commute was usually by a mini-van, or any car service that was available, and these were usually packed to capacity. On many occasions, when they could not get a ride, Melody, her sister Bubbles, and other Sunday School-goers would walk most of the way, before they got a lift. As they walked along, Bubbles would ask Melody to wave down a passing car that looked familiar to them.

"Flag him down nuh, Melody. It look like Mass Ephraim. You little, so you do it. Him wi stop."

Since Melody hated walking, she obeyed her older sister and most of the time she was successful. When they went to church with their grandmother, they would all wait for the mini-van.

Overall, Melody had been very involved in church and even contemplated getting baptized once, at age eleven. However, she got cold feet, and told her grandmother she wanted to wait until she was sure, so that she would not backslide. Guided by her innate sagaciousness, Grannyma agreed not to force Melody to commit herself, until she was sure she was ready. She suspected Melody's enthusiasm, had been a reaction to the three-day revival conducted by the visiting ministers from Tampa, Florida. Grannyma had witnessed the baptism of many young people as a result of these revivals, and saw how after a couple of months, they would backslide and revert to their old behavior. She was even more appalled, to see how some of them, behaved worse than before they were baptized.

"You must know what you feeling Melody. Although you not too young to serve God, you nuh, because Samuel was only a little boy when the Lord used him". "But," Grannyma had emphasized, "at the same time, you might have revival fever and it might wear off, as soon as revival done. So I can only pray for you still, that one day, you will be truly ready to serve the lord."

Melody had listened to her grandmother's sage advice and just as she had said, three weeks later, Melody had found herself not to be as spiritual as she was, when the revival was in progress. However, she remained a devoted, regular churchgoer until the time she left for America.

* * * * * *

"Lord, oh! I better move it fast, the van will soon be here,"Melody says, glancing at the clock, as she prepares for church.

Both Bubbles and Roderick are not feeling well. She is not sure if her brother is faking, but she is certain that Bubbles is really ill. Bubbles has been experiencing stomach problems since the day after Thanksgiving and her mother has coaxed her into taking a laxative.

"Bubs, darling, I think you should take some *washout* before you go back to school. The body needs to be purged now and again."

So Bubbles had taken the laxative late Saturday night, before she went to bed. Mrs. Pennycook had bought some senna pad at the West Indian store on Flatbush Avenue and boiled it real strong for Bubbles. Melody gagged at the mere thought of the words senna and washout and hopes her mother will not include her in the torture of taking the l herbal medicine. She always hated to take "washout" back in Jamaica. Grannyma would coerce Melody and Bubbles into taking a washout every Summer. She always made a point of purging them with an appropriate home laxative before they went back to school after the Summer holidays.

Melody, always the stubborn one, would give Grannyma a heartache every time she had to take her herbal medicine. Once, when she was given some castor oil (with condensed/sweet milk in her hand to disguise the taste), she gagged over the oil and spilled it. Grannyma was very upset and gave her a proper beating, because that was the last of the oil, she had that day.

Melody believed that, in America, she would be free from this Jamaican ritual, and was surprised when her mother brought home the familiar bush. "Oh bwoy!" she had said, "mi never know sey them have this sorta thing over here. Mama not going to know when me have stomachache atall!"

Melody hastens to finish getting dressed, happy that she is not sick. Today, she is even prepared not to complain about the cold and is determined to go to church against all odds. At least the commute to church in America is much easier than it was in Jamaica. She doesn't have to walk or take a mini-van because she is picked up by the church bus every Sunday. And, if she does not want to stay for the morning service, the driver is willing to take her home after Sunday school. Many times, she does stay for the service, while Roderick and Bubbles go home after Sunday School, unless she pleads with them to stay with her.

"Cho, man, stay nuh, and listen to the choir. Them sing good, man," she would say.

The church, The Solid Rock Pentecostal, has a mixed membership of African Americans, some Caucasians and West Indians. The pastor is American, Reverend Lovelace. Melody is very impressed with the choir. The first time she heard them sing, she found herself on her feet moving to the beat. "Mmmm, Americans can really sing good, eh? Look how them take a simple song (the rendition was, <u>On Christ the Solid Rock I Stand</u>) and make it so pretty. Bwoy, mi never know sey them can sing so good," she had thought, and looked forward to hearing them each time she went to church.

The choir is made up of mostly Americans, with a few West Indians, mainly Jamaicans, who have adapted to the American-style of singing. Melody is fascinated by the lead singers in the choir; they are either quite chubby or real petite. Many times, she has felt her body shake uncontrollably, as if she is 'getting into the spirit', when the choir sings. But, she still does not want to make a commitment. She has made a decision to just continue to go to church as long as she has the opportunity to do so.

A Feeling of Belonging

Monday morning seems to come quickly. After the long, four-day Thanksgiving break from school, Melody must face another week of new experiences and challenges. The small alarm clock on her bedside table chimes, awaking her from a dream. She was dreaming that her last class was being dismissed, the bell had rung, and she had not finished taking down the notes from the board.

The ringing sound in the dream hinges on reality, because Melody soon becomes aware of her ringing alarm clock. She yawns lazily and stretches, turning the radio dial to 1010 WINS to listen to the weather forecast. As she gets out of bed and walks towards her closet, the newscaster says: "This is 1010 WINS, YOUR NEWS UPDATE AND WEATHER STATION. IT IS 25 DEGREES IN THE BIG APPLE. HIGHS TODAY, 35 DEGREES. THE WINDS ARE CURRENTLY GUSTING AT 30 MILES PER HOUR. WITH THE WIND CHILL FACTOR, IT FEELS MORE LIKE 5 DEGREES. BUNDLE UP NEW YORKERS."

Melody rumbles through her closet to find a very warm outfit. She takes out her green corduroy jumper dress and a black turtle neck sweater blouse and rushes into the bathroom before Bubbles. Bubbles usually spends a long time in the bathroom fixing her hair in different styles before deciding on a style for the day. Her mother told her many times that she loves to "titivate up" herself too much.

After getting dressed and eating the cornmeal porridge their mother has prepared, Melody and her siblings venture out into the brisk Monday morning weather. By the time she gets to the schoolyard, Melody notices that everyone is pacing in an effort to keep warm. She timed her arrival to get there just as the bell rings.

The curriculum for the second marking period is a little more advanced in all the subjects, but Melody refuses to be intimidated. After class, Mrs. Varma calls to her, as she is about to walk out the door.

"Melody, just a minute, I need to speak with you."

Mrs. Varma pulls out a large brown envelope from her attaché case and hands it to Melody. Melody looks at the words "Writing Symposium – December 5th" on the envelope, as she takes it from her teacher.

"I will give you more details about this, soon," Mrs. Varma advises her.

Mi Neva Know Sey

The trip is less than two weeks away. Melody experiences a spontaneous joy and anxiety when she thinks about going to the nation's capital. She still cannot believe that she has been selected to represent her school; after all, she is only a newcomer both to America and the school. She continues to stare at the envelope as she nears her locker to retrieve her math book. Melody barely notices Wanda in the hallway talking with Jerron, Melody's classmate. Jerron and Wanda both look at Melody furtively, and continue to speak coyly. Melody braces herself to ignore them, as she quickly retrieves her book and closes her locker.

"Hey M-e-lo-dy whatsup!" She is startled when Jerron calls out to her.

"Hi, Jerron." Her response is unaccommodating. She suspects that Jerron is conspiring against her with her adversary, Wanda. She turns and walks away, wondering if Jerron and Wanda are not going to class. It is only a couple minutes before the next period begins. She smiles to herself, realizing that Jerron usually does not attend many classes. She previously had inferred, whenever Jerron was absent, that he was not in school. Now seeing him, and being aware of his lack of motivation, Melody suspects that he must regularly plays *hookey* from class, and hang out in the hallway.

Math class is very difficult. The class is learning pre-algebra and Melody is trying to understand all of the equations and symbols. About five minutes before the period ends, Jerron walks in, gives Mr. Shakall a note, and goes to his seat.

Melody gives a sniffling smile. "Is why 'im bother to come to class now. I guess because him know seh mi see him. Well, they say "better late than never!"

Jerron catches up with her on her way to her third period class.

"Hey, Melody, whatsup! Can I talk with you while you walk?"

Melody rolls her eyes, loathingly, and wonders what he wants to say to her.

"Hi, Jerron," she mumbles. "If you can talk fast enough. I am on my way to my next class, as you can see. I am not like you."

"Come on, Melody, what is *that* suppose to mean?"

He pretends he does not know what she is alluding to. Melody gives him a Grannyma look of "don't form the fool with me bwoy. You know what mi mean."

"Come on, Miss Wiz. Don't be giving me the cold shoulder. I ain't just messing with you for nothing."

Jerron does his hip-hop walk as he speaks.

"See, Miss Wiz. I be watching and listening to you in class for a long time. And I know you smart and all. You see, I need you to help me out with my school work. Melody, you from Jameka, but you real smart."

Melody looks at him, curiously, as she thinks, "So what? What does that mean?" But she does not say anything.

Jerron continues. "Yea, Melody, next year, I be going to High School and I need you to help me with my English. So what you say, Miss Smarty, can you help a brother?"

Melody gives a big sigh. "If you really need help, I guess I can help a little. But why me? I am new here. Can't you find someone else? What about the teacher?"

"Mrs. Varma! I know you wouldn't understand." Jerron seems embarrassed.

Melody is being extremely careful not to jump into this situation. It strikes her as funny how she has known this boy since September and he has never asked for help until now. She tells him yes, yet she is not sure how they are going to accomplish the task.

"And when and where am I going to tutor you, Mr. Jerron? Do you have any suggestions? I do not."

"Well, I was thinking if you ask your Mama and I come to your house, or sometimes in the cafeteria when we eating lunch."

"My house! I don't think so."

"Come on, Melody. Please ask your Mama." He looks desperate.

"Okay, I will. But I hope you coming just to let me help you, ahoa!"

Jerron laughs. "Hey that's a neat word what you just said, 'ahoa'. Is that a Jamekan word?"

Melody ignores him. "I will let you know what my parents say."

"Thank you, my sistah. Really appreciate it."

* * * * * *

On her way home from school, Melody remains preoccupied with Jerron's proposal. The "be careful" trait that her grandmother instilled in Melody and her sister resurfaced. All kinds of thoughts plague her mind, enhanced by the fact that she saw Wanda and Jerron conversing together.

She hates feeling this way, but it is a part of her personality.

"Always look before you leap!" Grannyma had told them.

On the other hand, Melody feels good about helping out a fellow classmate. This is not the first time she has found herself in this situation. She actually was an unofficial private tutor to a girl back at Chenrt School, a year before she left Jamaica.

Duhania Savetry, was an East Indian girl,(commonly called a coolie, in Jamaica) who befriended Melody and relied upon her for help with her writing. Duhania had a slight impediment, a cut in her top lip that caused a slur in her speech and made her uncomfortable and conscious of her defect. Without any regard for Duhania's feelings, her insensitive schoolmates gave her a nickname and teased her heartlessly. She was called "Lippy," and many speculated that her mother must have been cutting a piece of meat when she was pregnant and rested her hand on her stomach. They claimed this resulted in Duhania's deformity. It was her birthmark, according to them.

Melody never followed the crowd. She was sensitive to Duhania's plight and they had become friends. Duhania's family was well off. Her father owned a small supermarket, so Duhania always brought a lot of lunch money to school. With Melody's ability to write well from an early age, she was able to assist her friend in her assignments. Melody's philanthropic deeds were often rewarded with an American apple or other gifts from Duhania. As she reflects on this, she views Jerron's request more positively.

* * * * * *

Although it is not as windy as it was when they walked to school, it is still cold, so Melody walks hurriedly home, as Roderick promenades behind her.

"Good evening, Mama," Melody greets her mother, as she walks in the door. Mrs. Pennycook is off from work today, so Melody can discuss Jerron's proposal with her later.

"Good evening, Melody . . . Roderick."

Mrs. Pennycook is watching the last five minutes of her soap opera, "Days of Our Lives." She responds to the children passively. Roderick goes directly to the kitchen as usual, and snacks on cookies. Melody goes to her room. She feels exhausted and will use the time to relax until, her mother is finished watching her show.

Having returned to school after a long holiday brings to mind her first week at school in September. Soon, she hears her mother laughing and talking to herself, which signals the end of the program. She is anxious to get this matter over with, so she returns to the kitchen to speak with her mother.

"So, Melody, how was your first day back at school, today, after your short break for the Thanksgiving?"

"A'right, Mama. But we have a whole heap of new work. And it kinda hard. But I am going to try my best, Mama."

"Good, me love. I know you will try you best."

"Mama, this boy in my class wants me to . . . ."

She stops short, as her mother gives her a questioning look, then continues after regaining her composure. "Jerron in my class asked me to help him with his school work, especially English. Said I am smart and he doesn't want to ask Mrs. Varma. I told him I would check with you first." She tries to get it all out in one breath.

"Want you to help him, um! You sure is only that him want you to do? Him new to the class?"

"No, Mama." She knows her mother would be curious.

"So why him just asking you?"

Melody smiles inwardly at her mother's curiosity and she recalls the old proverb. "Chip does not fall far from the block." Her mother's reaction is just like hers, but she is going to circumnavigate the question. The truth is, she feels flattered that Jerron asked for her assistance -- this promotes her sense of belonging – that she is fitting into the American mainstream. Inwardly, it makes her feel good because she is being placed in a positive situation in her new school life.

"No, Mama. He is not new but I guess he is not catching on."

"So, where you going to do this tutoring, Mel?"

"Maybe here, Mama, and, sometimes, at school." Her heart is beating rapidly.

"Um!" Mrs. Pennycook pauses. "I will mention it to your father but I think it will be a'right, as long as he can come here when Wintson or me home."

"Thanks, Mama," Melody gives a sigh of relief, as she returns to her room. She is shocked that her mother agreed to have Jerron come to the house. "Bwoy look like it easier to talk to parents in America. If it was Grannyma, I know the answer would be no."

In Jamaica, Melody and Bubbles had very little privilege of inviting any boys to their home, especially Bubbles, who is older. Grannyma was more than strict with them. She was tough and always reminded them that she was not going to allow Miss Nel to blame her for anything that went wrong with them. Melody is relieved that her mother gave her the okay, but she is still apprehensive about Jerron's proposal.

"I only hope he will catch on quickly because me not taking a long time to do this. I will tell him tomorrow when I go to school."

She picks up her history book to start her homework before dinner is ready. She has a lot to do, because all the teachers have given homework, without any regard for their students' work volume.

* * * * * *

At school the next day, Jerron walks over to Melody's lunch table where she is sitting alone. Kirk and Ariel have had their own schedule lately. "Whatsup, Melody! Did you check with your folks?"

"Yes, I did." She detests his greetings.

"So what's the word?"

She hesitates, then responds with a question. "How long am I going to be tutoring you, Jerron? I hope it won't be a long time 'cause I need to keep up with my work too."

"Is that a yes? Hey, a man cannot be too greedy. Maybe four, five times. Maybe less. Thank you. When can I start?"

"We could now, but I don't believe you are ready."

"Come on, Miss Smarty, don't be so serious. How about tomorrow, right here in the cafeteria."

"Fine. You can only come to my house when my parents are home."

"That be alright with me. Remember I only live around the block from you."

Jerron walks away slapping his two hands together and rubbing them in an assured manner, as if to say: "mission accomplished." He saunters back to his table where his buddies are seated to finish his lunch. A loud burst of laughter fills the cafeteria; Melody looks up and sees Wanda and her friends talking, laughing and looking at the table where Jerron is sitting with his friends. They are extremely noisy, which brings the lunchroom teacher to their table. She asks them to quiet down, however, as she turns and walks away, the noise increases again.

Melody shakes her head in contempt and goes back to minding her own business. She finally has time to read the information Mrs. Varma had given to her regarding the writing contest. She learns that another student from the primary grade was also selected to represent the school district. The symposium is divided into two categories to accommodate entrants from grades two to eight. Fletcher Stern is the chosen student from Mr. Rolyat's class at the Elementary School. The event will be held at the Cultural Center on Virginia Ave, in Washington, D.C. They will be staying at the Marriott Hotel adjoining the center. She and Mrs. Varma will share twin rooms at the Marriott and Fletcher and Mr. Rolyat will do the same. They will travel to Washington by Amtrak and will leave on Friday evening from Grand Central station, and return Sunday evening.

The bell rings for the next class before Melody is able to read all the guidelines for the contest. She folds up the long letter, replaces it in the brown envelope and puts it in her book-bag. She will finish reading the material when she gets home and show it to her mother and father.

Jerron, his group and Wanda and her friends have already left the cafeteria. Jerron approaches Melody when she enters the hallway. "Congratu-lations Miss Wiz. Told you. You smart." He is gesticulating as he speaks.

"Congratulations for what, Jerron?"

"Yea, right! You be acting modest and stuff. You cool, girl. Miss Jamekan. Is this the way all the chicks act down in Jameka?" He is now walking laterally, almost in front of Melody, as he speaks, to get her full attention. "Look over there and tell me what you see, eh, Miss Wiz."

He points to the big bulletin board outside the main office. Written in gold on a large piece of black construction paper is: "REPRESENTA-TIVES FOR WRITING CONTEST, DECEMBER 5TH, WASHINGTON, D.C. MELODY PENNYCOOK, 8TH GRADE; MRS. VARMA -- FLETCHER STERN, 4TH GRADE; MR. ROLYAT: (The Elementary School). LET US WISH THEM THE BEST OF LUCK."

Melody gasps. She is excited. She is now a public figure in the school to those who know her and others who will know her. She doesn't know how to handle this; she has always been a private person. Reticent is a better way to describe her.

"Oh!" She says to Jerron. "I guess the whole school knows now." "So we meet tomorrow. See you, Me-lo-dy." Jerron moves away, walking backwards, while still talking to her.

Melody's next class is gym, so she knows for sure she will not have Jerron in her class. She looks over her shoulders at the bulletin board and sees students lingering to read the announcement. Her heartbeat accelerates. Jerron and Wanda are talking again and pointing to the bulletin board. She immediately dismisses any and all negative thoughts and hurries off to her gym class.

* * * * * *

That night, Melody waits up for her mother's return from work. She had shown the letter to her Dad earlier, but wants to show it to her Mom, personally. She knows that it is up to her mother to assist her with the preparations for the trip anyway. After her Dad glanced over the letter (while watching television), he had given it back to her and mumbled, "Good, good, show it to you mother."

She allows her mother to relax and blow off, then they both look over the letter. Melody learns that the contest will start at 10:00 a.m. on Saturday morning and end at 2:00 p.m. A reception will follow where all the guests and contestants will have a chance to mingle and get acquainted. After the reception, there will be a break, and between 6:00 p.m. and 7:30 p.m., during dinner, there will be lectures from various journalists and authors. The letter also describes the topics and categories for the essays: each entrant will write two, four-page essays on their selected topics.

Melody and her Mom are overwhelmed, happy and nervous. A passing apprehension overshadows Melody. She experiences 'cold feet', but she in not going to back out now. She cannot disappoint her teacher and her school. Moreover, the adventure is an opportunity she does not want to miss.

Her mother hands the letter to her. "Go for it, mi child. You will make me proud if you do a good job. But just the fact that you get selected. I feel good, 'cause I was very, very concerned how you was going to fit into the American school."

* * * * * *

It is the middle of the week, two days before the school week ends, and Melody is impatiently awaiting Friday. She is having lunch alone, again. As she finishes her meal, Jerron strolls over to her table. He has his English notebook and textbook with him. Melody helps him with his comprehension and analogy -- these are the areas in which he says he is having difficulty. He also explains to her that he had trouble understanding the lesson earlier in the English class, so they go over the assignment together. Melody tries to explain the theory and he does an example by himself. He realizes that time is limited, so he tries hard to understand and follow her explanation.

Melody tutors Jerron for the rest of the week and he appears to be picking up quickly. Melody wonders if he was really in need of tutoring. He also tells her that he has problems with essay writing – that even if he thinks of a topic, he has problems expressing his thoughts and making the story flow. She promises that he can come to her house for help with that on the Saturday after she returns from D.C.

"Swell, Melody. This is great. How come when the teacher explains I don't get it?"

"Maybe you would get it, if you paid attention in class and ask questions if you don't understand."

Jerron walks away, hip hopping towards his buddies on the other side of the room. On the way, he stops at Wanda's table to whisper something in her ear. As she leaves the cafeteria, Melody turns around to look at Wanda's table just in time to see the two heads together. This closeness between Jerron and Wanda makes Melody uneasy. Why are these two such a twosome? What are they plotting? Melody shudders even at the thought.

Loving The American Adventure

On the morning of the trip to Washington, D.C., due to pure excitement, the day seems to drag by slowly for Melody. She finds it hard to believe that, later this evening, she will be in the nation's capital. Due to anxiety, her overnight bag has been packed since Wednesday.

As soon as school is dismissed, she rushes out the door for home. She sees her brother talking to his friends and gestures to him to come on.

"Cho, Melody, man!" Roderick has picked up this phrase that he had heard his family use so often. "Why you got to be rushing and it's Friday?"

"Catch you later, little brother. Number one, it is too cold for me. And I've got a train to catch." she responds, using her American accent, and hurries home to freshen up and wait for her teacher.

Roderick promenades behind her, muttering softly to himself.

* * * * * *

Melody had been in uptown New York (Manhattan) before; her previous trip was during the day, and had been by train. This trip is by car, which enables her to see more. The traffic this evening is congested. Mrs. Varma maneuvers her Cutlass Supreme through the crowded streets. It is rush hour, and the FDR Drive is busy. Mrs. Varma believed she had escaped the heavy traffic by using this route. After crossing the Manhattan Bridge to Canal Street, she takes the highway rather than going up Broadway to Grand Central Station. She assumed the route she chose was the quickest.

Melody admires the view along the highway: the East River with its beautiful boats, as well as the impressive skyscrapers. She sees the bridges that connect Manhattan to the Outer Boroughs, also the many other, interesting sites.

"So, Melody, here we are fighting our way in New York's Friday evening traffic. Is this how it is in Jamaica?"

"Uum ! Yes, Miss. I mean, I think so. Yes."

Melody is stumbling to find the right words because, in reality, back in Jamaica, in Spanish Town, she never had the experience of traffic jams, because she never rode in cars too often. Her response is based on what she heard about traffic problems in Kingston and the other cities.

"Excited?" Mrs. Varma turns to Melody, as she nears the station area.

"Yes, Miss."

"Well, Melody, I must say I am proud to have recommended you to the principal for this writing contest. You have demonstrated to me your writing abilities over the short time I have known you".

"Thank you, Mrs. Varma. I thank you, Mam."

"Well, I am sure you and Fletcher will do just fine. Hope they are here already."

The car pulls into Jerry's long-term parking garage, which is adjacent to the station. Mrs. Varma hands her keys to the attendant and receives her claim ticket. They take the elevator from the ground level to the first floor where Mr. Rolyat and Fletcher are waiting for them. Mrs. Varma purchases two round trip tickets, for Melody and herself. With tickets purchased, the four Brooklyn school celebrities find their way to the designated platform to await the arrival of the Amtrak Liner. They find a bench, which can seat all four, and sit down.

"Your name is Fletcher, right?" Melody makes conversation with her selected counterpart.

"Yea, right." Fletcher is not very friendly or garrulous.

"Are you nervous . . . excited, Fletcher?"

"Not really."

Fletcher only responds with short answers. Melody gets the message that he does not want to talk. She stops trying to make conversation. Her disappointment is short-lived as their train enters the station and they board it for their journey to Washington, D.C.

Melody and Mrs. Varma sit together, across from Fletcher and Mr. Rolyat. They converse for a good half of the journey. Mrs. Varma then starts to read her book and eventually falls asleep. Melody glances at her other traveling companions. Mr. Royalt is already nodding and snoring, quietly. Fletcher sits beside him like a zombie, staring into oblivion.

"Bwoy, him don't look friendly, atall. Anyway, to each his own, better him quiet than being like Miss 'tegereg' Wanda," Melody consoles herself.

She resorts to reading her novel as the train picks up speed, heading south. Soon the Big Apple (New York) is behind them and, every time the conductor announces a stop, Melody peeks out the window to read the name of the station. Somewhere between New Jersey and Northern Philadelphia she begins to feel drowsy and drifts off to sleep, but is jarred awake each time the train pulls into a station.

When she becomes hungry, she pulls out the bun and cheese her mother made for her from her tote bag and eats it, quietly. Mrs. Varma is still sound asleep and Melody is careful not to disturb her. Melody assumes that because of her age -- early fifties -- Mrs. Varma must be very tired after a week of teaching. Although only a student herself, who finds school life very tedious, Melody can imagine what it is like for the teachers who are loaded down with many responsibilities.

She resumes reading her book but, within an hour, the conductor announces the next stop – "Union Station, Washington, D.C." Melody nudges her teacher with her elbow, "Miss, I believe our stop is next."

Mrs. Varma wakes up and tries to focus her eyes out the window. "I am sorry, Melody . . . didn't mean to abandon you at all. I must have slept all the way, huh?"

"That's okay, Miss. Don't feel bad. I slept a little too."

Mr. Rolyat is awake, too; his eyes are red like fire. He is not embarrassed and does not apologize to Fletcher. The train pulls into the station and all four disembark. Melody is awestruck by the vastness of her surroundings. She still cannot believe she is in Washington, D.C. and silently repeats her favorite line, "Bwoy mi never know sey, mi would live to come know such a famous place."

She had seen the city on television many times and is aware that it is a very important place in America. It contains the home of the President of the United States of America -- The White House -- and many other famous buildings and landmarks. She is excited. She likes this aspect of being in America. As a matter of fact, she enjoys many things outside of the school premises and reckons that America is not so bad after all.

When they arrive at the hotel, a short distance from the train station, Melody is overwhelmed at its ambiance. A queen-size bed is all hers in this beautiful, magnificent edifice. She slaps her chest hard with her hands. 'Mi have to write Retti and tell her   'bout this. Bwoy mi have to say it again. Mi never know sey I would live to come see this. Mi little half and half Jamaican brown skin gal. Miss Lilieth granddaughter, you can't fool youself. You love this. And if it wasn't for troublemaker Miss Wanda she, I could say America is like paradise and I love it so far."

She unpacks her overnight bag and sets out her accessories on the big oak armoire, with its mirror detached and hanging from the wall. In a couple of hours, she would meet the other contestants for a light snack before retiring to bed.

* * * * * *

The following morning, Melody is alarmed when the telephone rings. It is Mrs. Varma calling from the next room to see if she is up. Although it took her a while to fall asleep during the night, she was finally able to do so by watching a movie on television.

"Yes, Miss, I am up."

"Breakfast is at 9:15 a.m. I will get you when I am ready."

"Okay, Miss."

After breakfast, the representatives from Brooklyn join the other attendees in the huge convention hall. It is packed with youngsters of various races and age groups. Melody feels a surge of trepidation pass over her, but maintains a brave composure. Both Fletcher and Melody are directed to their respective seats and, when everyone is seated, the facilitator explains the rules. The competition begins.

Melody scans the topics and makes her two selections: "My School, My Community And Me" and "If I Could Change the World." She begins to write on her first topic: "*I am almost sure that this topic does not have to follow the sequence in which it is given and the author, left it up to the writer to use his/her imagination and creativity. Therefore, having said so, I will first rearrange the topic to express my thoughts – 'Myself, My School and My Community.' I do believe that the order of events of these three relationships starts with me and, although not a part of the topic, next comes the inter-relations with the family. As I begin to think more about this topic, a familiar cliche comes to mind -- A rhetorical question which is always asked – 'What came first, the chicken or the egg?'*"

Melody pauses and thinks for a while to get her thoughts organized. What she is about to express, has to do with her Christian belief. She knows that religion is not too openly expressed in America, and that there is no organized prayer in school. But, on the other hand, according to the American Bill of Rights, one has the right to express religious beliefs and civil acts; so she begins her essay again:

"*Although I am only thirteen years old and have not yet absorbed* all there is to know, I feel qualified to express my opinion on this question. I don't believe anyone should be doubtful of the sequence of the events when asked which was first. And I don't believe there should be any debate once one has read and believes the story of creation. At the young age of six years old, my grandmother taught me to read the Bible, and when I read Genesis, the story of the creation, explained that God created all things. The Bible was clear in stating that God made the animals, the fowl and other livings things -- both male and female. Ah! And I believe creating two different sexes was for a reason. So, from what I understood, the chicken was before the egg, as God did not say he made all eggs. Later, during the course of life, male and females reproduced in different species. However, since this essay is not about the creation, this is all I will say about this topic."

  By the time Melody is finished with her essay, she has written the required number of pages expressing all her ideas about "My School, My Community and Me." She then begins her second essay and finishes with the required number of pages. She reads over both essays, carefully, then hands them in and joins Mrs. Varma and the rest of the group in the lounge. The rest of the evening goes according to schedule and Melody feels special, as she moves around in her beautiful evening dress.

* * * * * *

  The train ride back to New York is not as adventurous and exciting as the trip down to Washington, D.C. Melody throws her head back on the cushioned seat and stares obliviously. She reflects on the weekend in the nation's capital. A passing thought flickers through her mind, intermittently – Did she write a good essay? -- She assures herself that she did her best.

  She thinks about a thousand different things, past, present and future . . . about going back to school on Monday morning . . . the reality of her new life in America. Wanda crosses her mind, too. But, just as quickly, she erases the thought of this girl who has had such a negative effect on her.

  Melody soon drifts off to sleep and is awakened only when the train jolts into slow motion, signaling its approach into a station. She opens her eyes and yawns, quietly, not wanting to disrupt her teacher. As she wipes the sleep from her eyes with her hands, she looks outside and sees familiar landmarks -- tall buildings, some burnt and marred, and in need of repair. Some with water discolorations and broken windows, leaving them open to the elements of the earth. There is no mistaking it – yes, she is back in New York – the walled city.

As the train throttles into Grand Central station, Melody notices that it is snowing lightly, and sticking to the ground.

"Well, we are home, again. See you Abraham. Bye, Fletcher! Hope you had fun." Mrs. Varma bids farewell to Fletcher and Mr. Rolyat, as she and Melody leave the station and make their way to the parking garage.

The ride home is slow -- not because of heavy traffic -- but because it is now snowing, heavily. After carefully wending her way through the snow, Mrs. Varma reaches Brooklyn and drops off her student.

Melody's family is happy to see her back home and share in the excitement, as Melody gives an account of her weekend trip.

"You come home, darling. How you spend you time?" asks her mother.

"Fine, Mama, real fine. Me never sey America so big and pretty. The hotel nice you see."

She retires to bed early in order to be well-rested for school the next day. "Another week of learning, homework and," she sighs, as she changes into her night clothes, "God only knows what else will cross my path."

The train ride home was exhausting, probably coupled with the stress of the writing contest. Melody drifts off to sleep in a short time and sleeps until the alarm clock rings at 6:30 a.m.

Coping With Jerron

"Hey Melodie whatsup! Miz ce-le-brity. How was the trip to D.C.?"

"Fine, Jerron. Fine."

"So we still on for this Saturday at your house?"

"This Saturday, what's with my house?" Melody has forgotten her promise to Jerron that he could come to her house for tutoring.

"C'mon, now Miz Wiz, you promised I could come for my tutoring."

Melody slaps her forehead with the palm of her hand. "Yea, I did promise, but today is only Monday. You took me by surprise."

She was not telling the truth. She actually hoped that Jerron had forgotten or would cancel the appointment. She is a bit annoyed, but a promise must be fulfilled. "Okay, Mr. Jerron, you can come at 1:00 p.m. on Saturday and I want you to know it will be the last time. I need to catch up with my own work."

"Cool, I understand."

School seems extra burdensome this week. On Friday, Melody wakes up to what appears to be a snowstorm and the news reports inform them that school is closed for the day because of the inclement weather. According to the weather report, snow will accumulate to six inches in the city and up to ten inches in the suburbs. This is the biggest snowfall that Melody has experienced since coming to New York.

"Bwoy, mi never know sey so much snow can fall one day, for real! Guess if it snows until tomorrow, Jerron will change his mind. There is something very strange about this tutoring, but I just cannot put my finger on it."

Melody is glad to be home from school. She finds a four-day school week very exhilarating. Her parents, however, are not that lucky; they had to go to work in spite of the weather. The day seems to go by slowly and Melody attributes this to the dismal weather. A look outside reminds her of the Christmas cards, her mother used to send them when she and Bubbles lived in Jamaica. Not too many people appear to be outdoors, today, but Roderick keeps asking her to go outside with him to throw snowballs and build a snowman.

"Cho, Roddy man, I will freeze to death. Are you crazy? Why you think school close today? It is because they know we will freeze if we go outside."

"Yea, right, Mel. Mom and Dad going to freeze? They went outside."

"Well, that's different!" She shrugs her shoulders and walks into the kitchen, where she secretly contemplates what it might be like to play in the snow. She wonders how the flakes would feel against her face and wants to roll a ball of snow in her hands. After all, to experience this new lifestyle would be a dream come true. The closest she had ever got to snow was seeing it on a Christmas card. She stands by the storm door in the kitchen and gazes at the snow with deep admiration.

"This is awesomely beautiful. God is really good. If I didn't come to America, mi woulda never know sey something else other than rain and sun rays come from the sky."

Overtaken and mesmerized by the enchanting view, Melody acquiesces to Roderick's nagging. "Wait first though, so I can pad up myself nice and warm."

The fun Melody experiences playing and gallivanting in the snow confirms her expectations. She is very happy, she was coerced by her brother.

By Saturday morning, over five inches of snow has accumulated. Nevertheless, by 12:45 p.m. Jerron shows up. His sneakers are covered with snow as he enters the hallway. Melody is surprised and annoyed that he did not use some wisdom and stay home because of the inclement weather.

"Phew! Santa Claus will be happy. He got snow for his reindeers. I love this Melody. They got snow in Jamekah?" Jerron exclaims, as he enters the house.

Melody rolls her eyes, showing the white of her eyeballs, and ignores his question. She reckons he is just trying to make conversation.

"I really thought you would change your mind about coming today, since it snowed."

"Naw! It doesn't bother me none. Plus, I can make one big step and I am here," replies Jerron, referring to how close he lives to her.

Melody's first impulse is to inform him that it is not okay to come to her family's house in this weather; but she does not. She wants to get this over with as quickly as possible. For the next half hour, Melody helps Jerron with his assignments and writing techniques, generally. She offers him a glass of carrot juice her mother had made (her grandmother had instilled in her that she should always entertain visitors). He loves it.

"Wooo! Never had this before. This is delicious. What's it call, again?"

Melody tells him the name for the third time. She is thrilled when the tutoring session is over and it is time for him to leave.

"I really appreciate this, Miss Wiz, honestly. It worked out pretty good for me although . . . ." He stops short, pauses and looks down at his Timex watch, impatiently. Then he looks over his shoulders and again fixes his eyes on Melody, strangely. He stutters as he attempts to complete his sentence: " . . . thanks, although . . . you . . . you don't like me, Melody." He is blushing.

Melody is not fooled. She senses that he is lying and wants to tell her something other than what he just blurted out. The curiosity is heart stifling.

"See yah, on Monday, Melody. Bye!"

As she closes the door, she hears someone shout Jerron's name. She pulls aside the door screen and sees Wanda and a friend standing on the curb. She is taut. Curious. Mad. Wanda lives two blocks from the Pennycooks. At this moment, Melody feels a sense of paranoia. Why is Wanda standing in front of her house?

"Cho, Melody, mind you own business. The sidewalk is free for all. Don't be so suspicious. Get a grip on youself," Melody scolds herself, as she closes the door behind her.

PART THREE

Enough Is Enough -- It's The Holidays

The streets and some of the buildings in Brooklyn are decorated with Christmas wreaths and other festive decorations. Two blocks from her school, at the door of the First National Bank, a female Salvation Army worker stands ringing a bell beside a large red iron pot that hangs from a chain. Her mission is to collect donations on behalf of her organization. Christmas is only a few weeks away and things seem to get more hectic as it draws closer.

Melody's school is no different from the other buildings in the neighborhood. Christmas decorations are displayed all over the school. Melody, Ariel and Kirk finally find time to have lunch together. It has been a long time since they have done so. Each has become involved in some personal endeavor that has limited their time together. Kirk is still active with the Drama club and is busy preparing for the Christmas play, while Ariel's new Dominican boyfriend has been occupying her time, both in and out of school. It is almost the end of the year, so they have a lot of things to catch up on.

After lunch, Melody bumps into Wanda on her way out of the cafeteria. She was not aware of Wanda's presence prior to the collision, and is convinced that Wanda bumped into her deliberately.

"Hey! Isn't this Miz Celebrity? And she thinks she better than everybody else. Yea, she think she is Miss Junior High School. But she is a thief, too." She eyes Melody, loathingly. "We gots to talk soon, you hear me, girlfriend. Gots to talk, real soon."

Melody Pennycook is shocked. *Angry.* In fact, she is furious. Since her last encounters with Wanda, she has mustered enough courage to confront her adversary, now. She is determined to put a stop to this nonsense before she leaves school, so that she can continue going to school in peace, the next six months.

"Thief! What are you talking about, Wanda?"

"Don't be acting all dumb like you ain't know where I am coming from. I see him coming from your house with 'ma own two eyes on Saturday."

"Gal, is wha you a talk 'bout? Back up little bit. Who is him?"

Mi Neva Know Sey

The Jamaican accent manifests itself and, for a minute, Melody does not care whether Wanda understands her or not. Then, she remembers the scene in Woolworth's at the Green Acres Mall between the Jamaican lady and the old clerk, and realizes that her performance is similar.

"I believe you *know* I am talking about Jerron."

Melody's heartbeat has accelerated. She now understands that Wanda is alluding to Jerron's visit to her house. She wants to be civil about this matter and attempts to explain to her adversary, but Wanda is already down the hall.

Wanda looks back at Melody and points her index finger, threateningly. "I'll catch up with you, Miss Jemaikan. You can bet on that!"

* * * * * *

Christmas is a week away. It is Thursday and school is dismissed early. School will be closed for two weeks, for Christmas recess. Quite a few students are carrying small gift packages wrapped in decorative Christmas paper. Roderick has two -- one from his grab bag and the other from Chantel, his friend, who has a crush on him. Melody has one -- it is from her grab bag exchange and she is not too crazy about it. It is only a Christmas tree ornament.

"Who tell this woman seh mi want this! Better she did give mi a pair of panty hose, I could use that."

This is her first experience with the school grab bag. She has learned a lot from this experience also. She had bought a cosmetic bag as her contribution to the grab bag -- something that any girl would like and could use. She realizes, now, that she had gone overboard.

No one seems to be in any hurry to get home. Students, in groups of twos and threes, are lingering outside the schoolyard. They are all very excited as they show off their gifts to each other. Melody also lingers, chatting with a few of her friends, while Roderick carouses with his buddies. Roderick has opened his gifts and is already playing with the toys he received.

However, if the truth was known, Melody is being accommodating to him. She would rather be on her way home.

"Hey, Roderick. Let's go. I am ready," she calls out to Roderick.

"Wait up, Mel. It is still early. Why the rush?"

"I am leaving!" she replies with determination.

At that moment, about ten steps in front of her, she sees Wanda showing off in a group of girls. She gives a big gulp and a lump sits in her throat.

"Oh no! Miss Tegreg." Melody recalls their most recent confrontation and the accusations Wanda made. She slows down, attempts to call back to her brother, then decides not to call attention to herself. She is annoyed that she cannot get Roderick's attention and keeps moving forward. When she is about two steps away from Wanda's group, Wanda calls out to her.

"Hey, Melody, Miss Jemaikan. You *just* rushing to get home, today, aren't you?"

Wanda approaches, as Melody advances. She feels a surge of anger and bitterness. She is afraid. She is not afraid of Wanda, anymore, but of her own reaction. It is not a good feeling. She has endured Wanda's taunts for a long time and she knows it is time to put an end to them. It is the season to be jolly and happy. . . A time of peace on earth. . . . But, ironically, for Melody, it is a moment of confrontation.

She does not like this feeling and wishes that Wanda would disappear and leave her alone.

"Miss oreo, salt and pepper. Don't you hear me calling you?" Wanda is beside her now.

Melody stops and faces her adversary. Her maroon ancestral blood surges through her whole body and she addresses Wanda in her deep Jamaican accent. At this moment, she could not care less, if Wanda understands her.

"Gal! Is wha you want? Wha you a badder mi fa? Mi trouble you?"

Melody's fair skin turns red and her cheeks are firm, as she bites her bottom lip with her teeth. "Wanda, let me tell you something." She begins to speak clearer now. "Please, get out of my way. I mean now; let me go home."

Wanda freezes. She didn't quite understand all the words, but she is sure of one thing, Melody is real mad.

"Excuse me! What did you say? Wait! Wait! Don't say nothing I don't understand. I gots something to say to you. Just because you think you so fine . . . light skin and all, your long hair, and you tall and all, he is mine! And don't be coming to my country to steal my boyfriend."

"Your boyfriend! Who! When!"

"I done told you the otha day. I sawed him and I am talking about Jerron. I sawed him leaving your house."

Melody gives a fake smile. "Jerron. Me and Jerron. Wanda, you have it all wrong. I was his tutor. He came to *me* for help."

"Yea! That ain't what he told me. Said you volunteer and he didn't mind, cause he wants the help."

"What! He told you that? Wait 'til I see him." Melody is now double mad.

"I don't care what you gotta do. Just stay away from Jerron."

Wanda moves closer to Melody and begins to point her finger in her face. "You come over here on your boat from your island and want to steal my property. Back off now or else . . . !" She stops short, when Melody exhales her breath in her face.

The Jamaican blood, now mixed with Irish blood, rekindles a second time. Her fair cheeks are like marshmallows roasting. She is angry. Steaming. Boiling hot. She drops her book bag to the pavement, grabs Wanda's fake leather jacket and pulls her close to her face. She groans. She sighs and groans again.

"Ummmm! Ummm! W-a-n-da. This is the last time you ever bother me. You see this face. Look good, gal. You see how red it is now. Red like fire. Fire burns. Wanda, I don't want to fight you. But I can't take it no more. You been bugging me ever since I came to school for no reason. As of today, Wanda, I am going to teach you a lesson."

Wanda tries to bite Melody's hand but Melody's long arm holds her firmly and pushes her against the fence.

A small crowd has gathered around them, including Wanda's friends. Wanda struggles to free herself and crouches to the ground, but Melody pulls her back to her feet. Melody bangs Wanda's short, stocky body against the fence several times and uses her head to lunge her adversary twice on her forehead. Wanda closes her eyes as she feels the pain and aims for Melody's wrist to bite her again, but Melody pulls Wanda's head back with her free hand. Wanda throws a punch towards Melody's stomach, but Melody turns sideways and the punch catches her at the side. Melody lowers her head to bang Wanda in her forehead again, while she is still pinned against the fence.

"Stop! Stop! You going to kill me?" Wanda yells.

Melody pauses and takes a deep breath. She pulls Wanda away from the fence and shoves her, causing her to lose her balance and fall to the ground. Melody stands over her saying, "Don't you ever . . . ," she bites her bottom lip with her teeth, shaking her head from side to side, and adds, "I mean . . . don't ever . . . come near me again. Like I said, this fire will burn you. Burn you real bad. Trust me, this is only the heat."

Melody is somewhat satisfied that she has taught Wanda a lesson.

But, to be sure it sinks in, she pulls her to her feet again and speaks closely in her face. "Let me tell you something. America is a free country. Your ancestors' ship stopped in America. Mine stopped in Jamaica. But our roots come from the same place. I do not want to steal Jerron. He is lying. Stay away from me. Do you understand me, clearly?"

She releases her hold and shoves Wanda backwards again, this time slowly. Wanda is shaking. She is speechless. Frightened. She moves slowly away from her opponent. Melody is still steamed up and feels the urge to lunge at Wanda again, but she maintains her composure and faces Wanda eye-to-eye for the third time.

"Wanda," she says, in an almost melancholy tone, "I came to America to experience a new life, like thousands of other people. And you know what? Before I left Jamaica, I had mixed feelings. I knew life here would be different and I came based on all the good things I heard about your country. But . . . ," she pauses and, without intending to, adds with a note of sarcasm, "you Wanda, put a bitter taste in my mouth. A problem I did not hope to experience with my own kind. Yes, I am black just like you, only a different shade. And one last thing, for the past six months, I have enjoyed many things living here. And Wanda, your attitude has boosted my appetite for America. It is a place I want to be and face future challenges. I feel sorry for you."

Wanda listens but does not respond. She is somewhat mesmerized and hypnotized by Melody's speech. Melody picks up her book bag and slowly begins her walk home. The crowd, including Wanda's friends, slowly disperses, looking over their shoulders as they leave.

"Hey, Mel, thought you reached home already. Whahappen! Holy smokes you are so red. Did you have a fight or what?" Roderick calls out, as he comes up behind her.

She does not respond; but Roderick sees Wanda and analyzes the situation. "Great, Mel! You did it! Bet she won't mess with you again." Roderick and his sister walk the rest of the way home in silence. Melody's conscience is mixed with satisfaction and guilt. Now, she is really looking forward to her break from school and hopes that the coming holiday season will bring joy to her heart.

* * * * * *

On Christmas Eve, it is very cold, with a marked briskness in the air. Last minute shoppers can be seen scurrying about in the snow, doing their last minute shopping. Everyone seems to be filled with the Christmas spirit. On television, Melody watches news reports of shoppers being interviewed at Saks Fifth Ave and Macy's. She is happy to be warmly huddled on her living room sofa, and not wandering around in the cold.

She uses this opportunity to recall Christmas in Jamaica. It was never cold. Cool, but not cold. Christmas in warm December. This brings to her mind a poem by Claude McKay, the Jamaican poet, who lived in Harlem during the Harlem Renaissance. In that poem, McKay spoke of the "poinsettias blooming blood red in warm December." Another thought about Christmas in Jamaica comes to mind, and it causes Melody to smile. "The only thing dem should abolish at Christmas time in Jamaica is de ugly something dem call Jonkanoo!"

It is Melody's first Christmas in America and, to her, it seems to be as exaggerated as the other American holidays. The festivities and the food are elaborate, but enjoyable. Since Thanksgiving Day was celebrated at the Pennycooks, Christmas is being celebrated at Aunt Pansy's. However, only the two families are celebrating together. No friends. No co-workers.

Aunt Pansy has an enormous Christmas tree located close to the window in her living room. Under the tree, there are lots of gifts. The curtains are pulled back on each side to display the tree to passersby. Melody does not overlook the fact that many of the neighbors have done the same thing. There seems to be some competition regarding who has the best Christmas decorations.

Melody cannot hide the thrill she feels as she experiences her first Christmas in America. She sits still for a minute, with a smile on her face, scrutinizing her surroundings. After exchanging elaborate gifts, the family enjoys a delicious meal and spends the rest of the day being jolly.

* * * * * *

The holidays seem to have come and passed, rapidly. Unlike Jamaica, there is no Boxing Day, (the day after Christmas) which is celebrated in Britain, and most former British colonies. For New Year's Eve, Melody was invited to the watch-night service at the Pentecostal Church she regularly attends. She accepted the invitation because there was nothing else exciting to do. New Year's Eve, she noticed, was a time for partygoers and those who can afford to dine out at the most exquisite restaurants. All the fun seems to end at 12:00 a.m., or later on New Year's Day. She had heard that many thousands of people trek into Manhattan to Rockefeller Center to see the fireworks display or to Times Square to see the ball drop.

Mrs. Pennycook was scheduled to work on both New Year's Eve and New Year's Day. Bubbles went to visit her girlfriend in Connecticut, so Melody was on her own, so to speak. She had overheard her father inviting a few of his friends over for the night and she definitely did not want to sit around the house with a bunch of raucous men. So, for these reasons, she opted to attend church on New Year's Eve.

Melody's plan was, to attend church, and return home by 1:00 a.m. She knew her mother would be home from work then. Moreover, the real reason she opted to go to church was to pray and seek God's protection for the New Year. Her fight with Wanda had left an indelible mark on her mind and, many times over the holidays, she had thought about their confrontation. Foremost in her mind, was whether Wanda was planning some kind of retaliation. Would Wanda get one of her friends to avenge her? Melody's conscience was also tainted with guilt. Had she overreacted to Wanda's annoying behavior?

The church service proved uplifting and spirit searching. The sermon seemed to be directed at Melody. At least, so she thought. The Reverend Jasper Lovelace's exact words were: *"The man who penned the words of this song, 'How I got over, my soul looks back and wonder, how I got over,' knew what he was talking about. Yea, brothers and sisters, the old year is passing. In a few hours, it will be a new year. And I knows it is God that done brought us this far. He the one that been by our sides all through the year, whether you be old or young, male or female. Yea, brothers and sisters, continue to trust God to he'p you in this coming year. He never change. No sah. No, no, not my God."*

Melody had listened and embraced the words for herself. There and then she decided she would trust God to make it through the next six months in Junior High... and even high school, when that time came.

When the Rev. Lovelace had given the altar call (an invitation for those who needed prayer to come forward), Melody was among those who responded. At the altar, she had prayed and asked God's forgiveness for her behavior, and for His guidance through the coming year.

Overall, she had enjoyed the holiday festivities and her first Christmas in America with her family.

A Pleasant Beginning

The holidays are over and the new school term has begun. On the first day back to school, the temperature is below 15 degrees. The students, who are lined up waiting for the bell to ring, shiver as they wait to enter the school building. Those who received new clothes and winter coats for Christmas, occupy themselves with showing off these items to their friends. Melody, meanwhile, is convinced that this is the coldest day she has experienced since the winter began.

The routine this term seems to be the same. Classes are no different from last term: the syllabus, however, has changed. The teachers are the same, but the student population seems to have changed at school. There are new faces around and some of the familiar faces are gone. Melody learns that some of her friends relocated to Queens and the Bronx. Jerron had moved, and transferred to another school in the Bronx. But, unfortunately, her adversary, Wanda and her group of friends are still in school, and will be in the same graduation/ promotional exercise with her in June. Melody was told by Brooke, that although Wanda is now in Seventh grade, she would still graduate in June.

This will be a short school week, since school reopened on Wednesday. At the end of the week, Melody receives the shock of her American life. As she sits alone at lunchtime in the cafeteria, she hears, "Happy New Year, Melody!"

She looks up to see Wanda, standing over her, smiling. Melody is paralyzed. Frozen. "Is this for real," she wonders. Can she take Wanda's demeanor at face value? Or should she be cautious. She chooses the latter.

"Hi Wanda," she replies, with an expressionless face.

"Yea, I know you wondering and everything. But I ain't come to bother you, Melody. This is a new year and I am a new girl. . . . Well my mind be new," Wanda looks down at the floor while talking.

Melody finds it hard to believe this is the same person she had the confrontation with a few weeks ago.

"Yea, that's right. I come to make peace. To apologize. I am sorry about everything. I guess I . . . ," Wanda stutters, " I guess I was just jealous of you. Ah mean just angry because you a Jemaikan."

Melody listens intently, without saying a word. Wanda continues.

"And you know what, that stuff with Jerron. It ain't true. We set this up together so I coulda 'ave a reason to accuse you."

Melody's semi-hazel eyes widen. The coincidental meetings between Wanda and Jerron are now clear to her. She swallows her saliva and makes a gulping sound, as she waits for Wanda to continue.

"I really didn't think about alla this you know. It just happened. Or maybe I still be mad about something."

Melody is at full attention now. She can't wait to hear what was the something that pushed Wanda to dislike her.

"You see, my ole man, ah mean my Daddy. Well he ain't my Daddy no more, 'cause I ain't seen him in a while. He left me and my Mama for a Jemaikan girl and they moved to Philadelphia."

"Umm . . . um! You never see smoke without fire," Melody thinks, as Wanda confesses.

"The way how you stood up to me, Melody, I know you ain't the one to be messing with. Can't lie. Girl, you were mad and I learn my lesson . . . and girl, if you had hurt me, I'd 'ave nobody to blame. I know you be laughing in your heart right now. But I just need to clear my conscience. That's it." Wanda finally got it all out.

Melody forces a smile. What more can she say, when Wanda relented in such a humble way. Melody is convinced that her victory and deliverance, so to speak, can be attributed to the prayer she prayed at the watch night service on New Year's Eve.

"Wanda, thanks for coming to me. Let by-gones be by-gones. And, by the way, I am not a regular fighter, but one got to do what one got to do to survive. You know what I mean. Let's put all this behind us now."

Melody now recalls what her mother had told her when she first started school in September. She smiles guilefully, knowing she had utilized the advice, she received. Both girls hug each other, not caring who is looking, after which Wanda leaves.

* * * * * *

For the rest of the school year, Melody is more relaxed. She does well academically and socially. In February, just before Valentine's Day, she learns from Mrs. Varma, that she placed second in the writing symposium. She is elated, although she did not come in first place.

"Second. That no bad at all, considering the amount of schools that me did see there." She predicts that her Mom and Dad will be pleased as well, and will share the good news as soon as she sees them. During the graduation promotions in June, she will receive her certificate of merit; the school will receive $500.00. Fletcher, she learns, placed tenth in his category and will also receive recognition.

By May, a few weeks before graduation from Eighth grade, Melody is informed by her guidance counselor that she will be promoted to the Ninth grade honors class in most of her subjects, including English. It is early, but she is already looking forward to her freshman year in high school.

Melody wonders what the coming summer will be like. She considers the pending summer her first real summer vacation in America. She now sees herself as grounded in the American experience as a result of her travails since emigrating. No it did not take her a long to learn the ropes about life in school in America. She had to, to survive.

"Me never know seh me would survive this far," she thinks, as she sums it all up.

Melody never told her mother about the fight with her Wanda, but Mrs. Pennycook is also happy that her daughter has made it this far. Her Melody, who she was so worried about, had made it through the transition. She is proud. High school will be another stepping stone, but right now she is enjoying her daughter's moment of accomplishment. She will cross that bridge when she gets to it.

* * * * * *

On Promotional Day, the auditorium is packed to capacity with the graduating class, parents and friends. The Pennycooks are proud of their daughter as she receives her awards for academic achievement. Their elation is apparent as they stand and cheer her as she walks across the stage to accept her awards. Their cameras capture the memories of this special day.

After the graduation exercises, Melody takes pictures with her friends, including Kirk. The family later dines at one of the restaurants featuring Jamaican cuisine, in Manhattan. Melody registers all these happenings in her mind. She will write to Grannyma and her friend Retinella and tell them about everything. Of course, she will include pictures.

A Spiritual Awakening

Melody opens her eyes, and tries to focus them to her immediate surroundings. She blinks several times, as the hot July sun pierces through her window, directly on her face. She closes her eyes for a second again, her long eyelashes resting on her lower lid. She is both happy and scared.

"The Lord is my Shepherd," she whispers, quietly, barely moving her lips.

She glances at the alarm clock. It is only 6:00 a.m. on Saturday. She sits up in bed, her back against the wooded bed frame, her long legs stretched out and her hands resting in her lap. She recalls the dream she just had. It was a spiritual one, more like a vision – that's what her grandmother used to call them. Melody remembers the Bible story of Samuel and is convinced that, through this dream, God is speaking to her just like he did to Samuel.

In her dream, she had started high school, the same one Bubbles attends. She was very excited and happy that she is now in the same school with her sister, although not for long, and a sudden fear came over her. She is walking to school with Bubbles, then the scene changes and she finds herself back in Jamaica. It was her baptism day, and she is on her way to church with Grannyma. She is dressed in white. When she arrives, Pastor Lattibeaudere, along with a group of church mothers, greet her and then they all go to the nearby river. At the river, she is taken into the water and baptized by Pastor Lattiebaudere. After the baptism, she looks around, but the crowd has disappeared and only one person is standing beside her.

Believing it is the pastor, she is about to ask him where her grandmother and the rest of the congregation went, but she cannot see the person's face. It looks like a man, dressed in white. He says to her, softly, "I will be your Shepherd." Then he leads her out of the water. At this point, the scene of the dream changes again. She is back in Brooklyn, at the high school she will be attending in September.

As she sits in bed, reflecting on her dream, Melody looks across the room at Bubbles, who is sound asleep and snoring loudly as usual. Her attempt to go back to sleep fails, so she gets out of bed and gets her Bible. She turns to Psalm 23 and begins to read. She reads the well-known Psalm a few times, repeating the first line, "The Lord is my Shepherd, I shall not want." The more she reads it, the clearer its message becomes. Warm teardrops trickle down her cheeks and fall on the page of the Bible. "That was God Himself in my dream," she thinks. "He will be my shepherd in high school. This is too plain a dream and I know what it means."

She places the Bible on the table next to her bed, lies down with her face buried into her pillow and quietly sobs as she falls asleep.

Later that afternoon, Melody shares the dream with her Mom and announces her decision to be baptized and commit herself to serve God. She had become a regular Sunday School member at the Solid Rock Pentecostal church, attending most of the special services. She will soon be an official member, and she suspects the Pastor will be happy.

"Well, Mel, Mel darling, I can't say I am not happy to hear your decision." Her mother responds, skeptically, as she flips over the red snapper fish she is preparing for dinner. "I kinda see it coming, the way how you love going to church. But is one thing I want to know, that you serious and know what you about to get into."

"Ye... Yes, Mama, I am sure," Melody replies, nervously. She too, is concerned.

"Well, honey, let me know when the big day arrives, so I can request the Sunday off, if I am scheduled to work that day."

"Okay, Mama, I will let you know. First I have to talk to Pastor Lovelace, and I know that they have a counseling session first, before the baptism." Melody is more relaxed now as she speaks with her mother.

She walks back to her room deep in thought. She paces the room several times, and stares through the window, intermittently. The dream is at the forefront of her mind, and more and more she is convinced that she is doing the right thing.

"Bwoy, if nobody else is really happy, mi know for sure Grannyma is going to cry for joy when mi write and tell her." Melody smiles, as she recalls the first time she decided to get baptized, when she lived in Jamaica. She plans to speak with Pastor Lovelace when she goes to Sunday School on Sunday.

She is now even more assured that the rest of the summer will be stress free. Her dream was right on time because, although she has tried to ignore the anxieties of going to high school, they have popped up in her mind occasionally. Her cousin Delraya had shared some horrible high school stories with her, and she had detected that Bubbles, too, occasionally had problems.

While the dream is still fresh in her mind, Melody sits on the floor in a corner of her room and writes a letter to Grannyma telling her of the spiritual commitment she is about to make.

In Retrospect

A year after immigrating to America, Melody finds herself sitting on the front porch of her house, as she had done when she first arrived. "Thank you Jesus for bringing me this far. I did not know I would make it." She looks across the street and does not expect to see the man walking his dog or the many other scenes she focused on a year ago. Today, the scenes are internal. In her mind and her heart. There are beautiful scenes and ugly ones, but she tries to focus on all the good ones.

She admits now that coming to America was not bad at all. She likes the idea of having a phone in her room, the clothes she can buy in abundance, the food so plentiful and affordable. She has been to many places, Radio City Music Hall, trips to Rye, just north of New York City and Coney Island. The ecstasy of going to the Empire State Building on 34th Street and the adventure of going across the ferry to the Statue of Liberty, were enjoyable. Then there was her trip to Washington, D.C., to participate in the essay contest for her school.

"But Melody, you did act scared and fool fool though. Never want go up so high and never want to go on the ferry," she laughs at herself.

After climbing all those stairs to the top of Lady Liberty's head, although out of breath, she felt she had accomplished a great task. She had been afraid to look down, but that fear was coupled with exhilaration. She remembers also her first subway train ride up to Manhattan, with her cousin Delraya. It was a noisy, adventurous ride to Times Square, but that too was a new experience. That day, she observed a lot from the faces of the passengers, as she sat in the car beside Delraya, who constantly made loud popping noises while chewing on her bubble gum.

Melody's thoughts are interrupted when she sees a lady loaded with large plastic bags, talking to herself; picks something out of the neighbor's garbage and eats it.

"Me never know sey me would see things like this in America. But now me know sey poverty can be anywhere."

She returns to her reflections. The Statue of Liberty is indeed a significant landmark standing on the small island across from Manhattan -- in the East River. It is truly symbolic of America, the land of freedom and opportunity. Opportunity to all nations, colors and ethnic groups. Opportunity, oh yes, to many people of the Caribbean and other small

Third World countries. And, more personally, Melody concedes, it is a land of opportunity for her family. "God Bless America," she utters to herself.

She came, she saw and she learned. She hated, she loved, and every day brought a new experience. Melody still cannot help uttering her usual refrain, "Me never know sey."

Coming to America opened up many opportunities, in many different ways. She had visited other states and Canada. Her first visit to Canada with her family was an adventure in itself. It was a journey over 500 miles which took between ten to twelve hours through the night and into the morning, until they arrived in Toronto the next day, at noon. But she enjoyed the ride on the New York State Thruway. She loved the occasional stops at the rest areas, to eat, stretch their legs, gas up the car, as well as bathroom breaks. She enjoyed browsing in the souvenir shops and purchasing banners and other souvenirs to add to her growing collection.

She remembers well one particular rest stop in Rochester, New York, close to Buffalo, which borders America and Canada. It was 3:00 a.m. and she had a heightened need to use the bathroom. When she entered the ladies room with her mother and Bubbles, she was shocked to see the long line and had exclaimed, "Me Jesus! Is weh all them people going? Me never know sey so many people on the road at this time of the morning."

As the memories of the past year unfold, she recalls that in Jamaica, she had never done so much in such a short period of time. She had never traveled such distances. But then, she reminds herself that the island is small and one can only travel within its fourteen parishes. She has also realized that America never sleeps, especially New York City.

Life in America for Melody may have started out with deep apprehension, but she has gradually become a part of the culture. Initially, the use of the term "God bless you," when someone sneezed had disconcerted her, but overtime, she found that she did the same, responding with a thank you when she was "blessed".

She still has some work to do in memorizing the American National Anthem. She had stumbled over some of the lines at her Eighth Grade promotional exercises. She had no problem with the first and the last lines, but in between she did. When the principal had asked everyone to stand for the anthem, she stood up, rested her right hand on her chest and came out strongly with "Oh say can you see, by the dawn's early light, what so proudly we hailed . . . ." She had mumbled the other lines until the last line, "O'er the land of the free and the home of the brave."

On the other hand, she still hopes she will never forget the Jamaican National anthems. She loved them both: "I Pledge To Thee My Country" and "Eternal Father," which is the one mostly used. She begins to sing quietly testing her memory of the songs. *"Eternal Father bless our land. Guide us with thy mighty hand . . . ."* Yes, she does remember all the words but, then, she only left Jamaica a year ago! She, however, makes a promise that whatever it takes, she will never let go of the cherished culture of her homeland. Sometime during the summer, she plans to write two long letters, one to her grandmother and the other to her best friend, Retinilla Roper.

* * * * * *

The summer of '81 is already very hot and humid, although it is only early July. Having been through her first year in America, Melody has experienced all the seasons. She now compares this summer to the last. "Bwoy, America is from one extreme to the other. This really feel hotter than when mi just come. Or maybe since mi did just come up from Jamaica, meh never feel the difference then." She uses a piece of cardboard to fan herself, as she reflects.

She is seated on a lawn chair in the small backyard, trying to avoid the heat wave that has swept over Brooklyn for the past few days. She goes into the kitchen to fill her fourth glass of homemade ice tea (her mother makes delicious ice tea and she now loves it). She walks out to the backyard again, and then goes to the front porch.

"Phew!" she sighs. "Guess mi wi get used to this heat like everything else."

She stands on her porch and looks down the block, where the fire hydrant is located. A dozen or so children and some adults have opened up the hydrant and are standing in the path of the water gushing from the spigot.

"But anybody see mi dying trial doh eeh. A who authorized dem fe do that! Look how much water wasting pon the street."

Melody is truly appalled, but at the same time, she understands their plight. She stands on the porch for a while and vicariously enjoys the fun the children are having at the hydrant. An urge to join them sweeps over her, but she restrains herself.

Memories of Jamaica besiege her. Jamaica, an island in the sun, surrounded by water, with beaches galore, ready and waiting for the hungry bather. There are big trees, with their branches widely spread, to give the weary traveler shelter from the sun. There are coconut trees that yield coconuts with water to quench the thirst.

She finishes her ice tea and walks back to the backyard, where she sits in a cool spot. She hopes that nightfall will bring some coolness to Brooklyn.

The End

Afterward

Melody has survived the ordeal of having to leave her country. She misses her grandmother and her friends, but she has persevered. Her prospects are bright. She has learned the painful lessons of adjustment, but she is a bright student and will no doubt go on to accomplish great things. Hope springs eternal for her.

As an archetypal immigrant, Melody's experience is the experience of many, who for economic and political reasons, must leave their country of birth. In a general sense, the narrative captures the feelings and emotions of most, if not all immigrants. In a particular way, it speaks to the myriad of emotional highs and lows, hope and despair that young immigrants must come to grips with, after arriving in a strange land. In a real sense, however, it speaks eloquently of the ability of these young people to adjust, and not only adjust but to go on to even greater things.

It is the hope and prayer of the author that the young immigrants, and the audience at large, reading this book will take heart and not despair. Be strengthened, by the fact that in the end it will work out to the glory of God.

BY: BARRINGTON C. HIBBERT- AUTHOR OF FOREWORD

KEY GLOSSARY- DIALECT WORDS/PHRASES AS THEY APPEAR IN THE STORY

SAILOR- MARINE/OFFICER
PICKNEY-CHILD
GRANNYMA- AFFECTIONATE NAME FOR GRANDMOTHER
GO WEY-GO AWAY
SAILOR PICKNEY- CHILD BORN TO A NEGRO WOMAN AND WHITE MARINE OFFICER
SEY/ SEH -SAY
PON- ON
FE- YOU
NEGAR-NEGRO
PICKY/PICKY- KINKY/NAPPY COURSE HAIR
WA-WHAT
NUH- RIGHT/OK!
ONOO-MORE THAN ONE/BOTH, YOU ALL
DE-IS
GWING- GOING
DAT-THAT
'CUT THEIR EYE' - DIRTY/NASTY LOOK
DEM-THEM
DUPPY- GHOST
MEK-ALLOW/MAKE/LET
VERANDAH-PORCH
DAWG-DOG
ROCKSTONE- HUGE STONE
LICK-HIT
DEY-THERE
BWOY- OH BOY!
'BOUT-ABOUT
MI- I/ME/MY
AH- I
BAMMY- ROUND BREAD LIKE DOUGH(SIMILAR TO PITA BREAD)
MESELF-MYSELF
LAWD-LORD
WID-WITH
FAIR SKIN PICKNEY- HALF CAUCASIAN

GAL-GIRL
MEMBER-REMEMBER
CUNUMUNU- SILLY LOOKING/ MORE LIKE A PUPPET
ATALL- AT ALL
FAVA- (AS IN FAVOR) RESEMBLE
MAWGA-MEAGRE/SKINNY
FRAIDE/FRAIDE- VERY AFRAID
SAH/SAR -SIR
FA-FOR
BADDA-BOTHER
LAWKES MAN!-GIVE ME A BREAK
WEY-WHERE
DOH-THOUGH
CALALOO-GREEN LEAFY VEGETABLE
JONKONOOS- MASQUERADERS
MI WI - I WILL
MI DYING TRIAL- EXPRESSION OF SURPRISE/SHOCK/WONDER-MENT
CHO MAN!- EXPRESSION OF FRUSTRATION
MESELF-MYSELF
MASE-MASTER/MISTER
FE PEEP-TO LOOK
FASE- NOSEY/CURIOUS
"WHAT SWEET NANNY GOAT A GO RUN HIM BELLY- A JAMAICAN PROVERB-MEANS THINGS CAN BE OKAY FOR ONE NOW,BUT IT DOESN'T STAY THE SAME FOR EVER.
CERASEE- BITTER HERBAL BUSH
BLACKMINT- ANOTHER TYPE OF HERBAL MINTLEAF
HAR- HER
FROCK- DRESS
TITIVATE- FIX/MAKE UP ONESELF- TAKING TIME TO GET DRESSED
"SEH ME TOO BRIGHT" – FECITIOUS/BOLD
AHOA- OH!
"SENSEY FOWL" - PICKY, VICIOUS/MEAN
PUTUS- AFFECTIONATE TERM, SAME AS IN 'HONEY' 'DEAR'
HARBERDASHY- DRY GOODS STORE- SIMILAR TO WOOL-WORTH, FIVE & DIME